The Venetian

MISSING PERSONS
book three

The Venetian Policeman

m. e. rabb

speak
An Imprint of Penguin Group (USA) Inc.

SPEAK
Published by Penguin Group
Penguin Group (USA) Inc.,
345 Hudson Street, New York, New York 10014, U.S.A.
Penguin Books Ltd, 80 Strand, London WC2R 0RL, England
Penguin Books Australia Ltd, 250 Camberwell Road, Camberwell, Victoria 3124, Australia
Penguin Books Canada Ltd, 10 Alcorn Avenue, Toronto, Ontario, Canada M4V 3B2
Penguin Group (NZ), cnr Airborne and Rosedale Roads, Albany, Auckland 1310, New Zealand

Published by Speak,
an imprint of Penguin Group (USA) Inc., 2004

1 3 5 7 9 10 8 6 4 2

Produced by 17th Street Productions,
an Alloy company
151 West 26th Street
New York, NY 10001

17th Street Productions and associated logos
are trademarks and/or registered trademarks of Alloy, Inc.

Speak ISBN 0-14-250043-7

Printed in the United States of America

For Elizabeth Carlin Everett,
and in memory of
Kathleen Carlin

Missing Persons Case #4256721

Name: Jack Jenkins

Age: 21

Height: very tall

Build: hard-bodied

Hair: shiny, dark, touchable

Eyes: green and smoldering

General Description: Babelicious! Hot hot hot!

Last Seen: Venice, Indiana, June 2000

Suspected Location: Starring on soap opera or sitcom in LA? Singing on Broadway? Leader of rock band touring Europe? Who knows?

One

"So is he a good kisser?" I asked.

Sam scowled. "That's none of your business."

"Of course it's my business. You're my sister," I said.

We were sitting in our favorite booth at the Petal Diner on a Sunday night in November, eating a three-course dinner of pink beet-and-potato soup, roasted salmon, and cherry cupcakes with pink-rose petal frosting (Wilda, the owner and chef, was trying out a new pink menu)—all for $3.99. I'm mentioning the price because being from New York City, I never stopped being astounded by the value of things in Indiana. In fact, even after four months, most things in Indiana continued to astound me. Sometimes I'd fall asleep on the bus home from school and then wake up expecting to see sprawling cement and high-rises; I always flinched at the surprise of oceans of corn and the occasional yard sign shouting, RABBITS: PETS OR MEAT.

That night the Petal Diner buzzed with activity; Sunday nights were one of the busiest of the week, probably because it was the only place open on Sunday for miles around.

"Well, does he use more tongue or lips? Does he slobber?" I asked Sam.

"Slobber? He's not a puppy."

I shrugged. "Some guys slobber. Randy Chaefsky—"

She made a face. "Randy Chaefsky slobbered?"

I nodded solemnly. "It was grim. In fact—"

She shook her head. "Spare me the gory details."

Sam was closer to me than anyone in the world, but we'd never talked about guys that much, probably because there hadn't been that many guys in our lives to talk about. My physical experience with the less-fair sex was limited to one brief, random makeout session with Randy on the subway coming home from my old school, LaGuardia High School of Music and the Arts in New York City. I'd had dates with two guys since we'd come to Venice, Indiana—Troy Howard and Pete Teagarden—but neither date had resulted in the kind of passion you read about in romance novels. I hadn't even kissed either of them. Troy had turned out to be a philandering Neanderthal, and Pete, despite considering himself to be worldly and sophisticated, would probably pronounce bagel as "bagelle."

"You have to give me some details on Josh," I said. "Seeing as I have no love life whatsoever, I need to live vicariously through you. Does he call you his girlfriend?"

"Girlfriend? I don't know. It's only been a few weeks since I've known for certain he wasn't our cousin," she said.

Sam had met the guy she was dating, Josh Shattenberg, while we were attempting to solve our last missing-persons case—Josh's grandfather, Leo Shattenberg, had hired us and our boss, Gus Jenkins, to find Leo's old girlfriend. Because Shattenberg was our real last name, too, we'd thought that Leo and Josh might be our long-lost relatives. It turned out that they weren't, which was good since sparks were flying so noticeably between Josh and my sister that I couldn't keep myself from making hillbilly cousin-mating jokes.

We hadn't been able to come right out and ask Leo and Josh if they were related to us because as far as they and everyone else in Indiana knew, we were Sam Scott and Fiona (nicknamed Sophie) Scott from Cleveland. Unbeknownst to them, our real names were Samantha and Sophia Shattenberg, of Sunnyside, Queens. Our mother had died six years ago and our dad died earlier that summer, leaving our penny-pinching, morose step-mother Enid to inherit everything. Enid had wanted to separate Sam and me, and to ship me off to a godforsaken boarding school in the Canadian wilderness. To prevent that from happening, my sister surreptitiously transferred our dad's money into an account of our own, we fled New York City, and ended up here in Venice, Indiana, which calls itself the "Europe of the Midwest" even though most of the town's inhabitants have never ventured past Muncie.

Wilda came over to our table. She wore pink eye shadow and a necklace strung with little black cats resembling her cat, Betty, who was sprawled across the diner's welcome mat.

"Still no sign of Gus?" Wilda asked.

Sam shook her head. "He said he'd meet us here over an hour ago." Sam worked for Gus full-time at the

Jenkins Detective Agency, and I helped out after school and on weekends. Sam was seventeen, two years older than me, and should have been starting NYU this semester, but as part of our new identities, she'd become twenty-one and my legal guardian.

Sam glanced at her cell phone. "I keep trying Gus at home, but he's not there."

"Well, I guess I'll just give you these now. I've got one for Gus, too, but I'll give him his when he shows up." Wilda reached into her apron and fished out two turkey-shaped cards.

You are cordially invited to
Wilda's Twelfth Annual Turkeyluck Dinner
Thanksgiving Day
4 PM
The Petal Diner
Please bring a favorite dish to share

"Turkeyluck?" Sam asked.

"It's Thanksgiving, and a potluck, so years back Chester started calling it Turkeyluck, and well, the name stuck. I invite everyone in town who doesn't have a big traditional family dinner to go to—last year Gus, Fern, Ethel, Henry, Chester and his wife, and a few others came. I make the turkey and a few pies, and everybody else brings side dishes. Last year Ethel brought the most delicious corn dogs . . . Fern made some gorgeous Sea Foam Salad. I think Gus brought a cheeseball."

"We'd love to come," I said, though my voice hesitated, and it wasn't just due to the mention of a cheeseball, which for the uninitiated is like a miniature bowling ball of cheese rolled in nuts or bacon bits. The problem with Thanksgiving is that when you don't have a traditional family, holidays aren't the most carefree and enjoyable part of the year. It was hard not to think about our regular Shattenberg Thanksgivings, with our mom and dad. My dad always cooked a big turkey that we could never finish. Sam and I complained about the turkey à la king we'd have for the entire week afterward —we never liked it. Now I'd give anything for turkey à la king made by my dad. Why hadn't I appreciated it then? It seemed like such a luxury now to be able to complain about the food your parents make.

Wilda must have sensed my reservations because she said, "I promise it'll be a meal you won't forget. I'm going to—"

"Garçon!" a voice interrupted from across the diner, in an embarrassingly inept French accent. It was police officer Alby. He was sharing a booth with Agnes Leary, who owned the Romancing the Stone jewelry shop on Main Street.

"Just a minute," Wilda told him sharply. She looked back at us. "I'm glad you can make it. You'll—"

"GARÇON!" Alby's voice rang out, louder.

Wilda rolled her eyes. "I'll be right back," she told us.

I stared at Alby. He wasn't looking like his usual self. Alby and his brother Chief Callowe comprised the entire Venice police force, and Alby was generally known as the laughingstock of it. Tonight, instead of his usual blue uniform, he wore a green polyester shirt with a large gold chain dangling down his chest. He looked like a stuffed sausage in his tight black jeans. He handed the menu to Wilda. "Steak with cheese sauce, sides of bacon, sausage, baloney, three slices of American cheese, and extra mayo. No bread. No noodles. No potato. I don't even want to see any carbohydrates on the table."

"What's up with him?" I whispered to Wilda when she came back to our table.

"Atkins diet," she muttered. "No starches whatsoever." She rolled her eyes. "He's on this whole self-improvement kick. He moved out of his mom's house, got his own place, and carries around a backpack full of self-help books these days. The other morning he sat at the counter reading *Mars and Venus in the Bedroom.*"

"Eww," I said. The idea of Alby in bed was not what you wanted to think about while eating.

"Another time he was reading *Creating Respect: How to Get What You Don't Think You Deserve,*" Wilda said. "This diet is the worst, though. No bread! No potatoes! The other day he ordered my chicken fried steak and picked my prizewinning breading off it—it won first prize six years in a row at the Venice Founders' Day Festival, and he won't touch it." She shuddered. "I told him this diet isn't healthy, but he won't listen." Of course, Wilda had her own interpretation of *healthy.* If she'd invented a food pyramid it would have everything deep fried on the bottom, a layer of pies and cakes, a layer of coffee, and a layer of raw vegetables at the very top in the "use sparingly" category.

The bells at the entrance to the diner jingled and a dark form appeared in the doorway. It was Gus. At least, it was a form that somewhat resembled Gus. I'd never seen him look this awful before: he was pale and unshaven, and his hair stuck out in strange directions from his bald spot. He had dark circles under his eyes and looked like he hadn't slept all weekend. He hovered in the doorway, glanced over at us, and then tripped as he started to make his way over to our booth. Betty yowled and shot across the diner like a cannonball. Gus shouted a string of expletives.

"Watch your mouth! There are young people in this diner," Wilda yelled at him.

He brushed himself off and leaned against the doorway. "You gotta get rid of that cat." He wagged his finger at Betty. "It's a health hazard. Fleabag vermin in a restaurant . . . oughta be a law against that. I'm gonna file a formal complaint with the chamber of commerce when I get a chance."

His speech was slurred; his eyes were bright red.

"You do that, Gus," Wilda said.

"I'm going to," he said. "Don't think I won't."

Wilda rolled her eyes and made the rounds with the coffeepot. Sam and I rushed over to him.

"Are you okay?" I asked.

He grunted, put a hand to his forehead, and rubbed his eyes. I could smell the alcohol on him. "Look, girls, I'm not really up for this. I'm going back home," he said.

"Are you all right?" Sam asked. "You didn't show up for work Friday, and . . ." Her voice trailed off.

"I'll call you tomorrow," Gus said.

Sam and I didn't know what else to say. We watched him turn and limp off down the sidewalk.

When he was out of sight, I asked Sam, "What's wrong with him? I've never seen him look this bad before."

Sam shook her head. "I don't know. He started acting weird on Thursday. He was in the worst mood and kept growling orders at me for no reason, then finally apologized and said he didn't feel well, and went home early. Then he didn't show up Friday, and this morning was the first time he picked up the phone. He sounded a little better then, like he was looking forward to meeting us tonight."

Wilda put the coffeepot back on the counter and started wiping it down. She'd heard our conversation and was smiling artificially, as if there was something she wasn't telling us.

"Do you know what's wrong with Gus?" I asked her.

She paused. "Mmmm," she grunted.

"What?" Sam asked. "What's going on?"

"Well—" She moved to the cash register and ran her finger over the Frolicking Felines calendar beside it. Each month showed a picture of a cat in different outfits; November was a tabby in a spacesuit. She rested her finger on Thursday, November 6, three days before.

"Yup, just what I thought," she said. She lowered her voice and spoke out of the corner of her mouth. "Thursday was *jick joookins* birthday."

"What?" I asked. She'd whispered the name so quietly I couldn't make out what she said.

She looked around to make sure no one was listening, and then waved us toward a deserted booth on the other side of the diner.

"It was Jack Jenkins's birthday," Wilda said.

"Who?" Sam asked.

Wilda folded her hands. "Gus's son."

Two

"Gus's *what?*" I sputtered. Sam's mouth opened. We'd known Gus had an ex-wife who'd left him several years ago, but no one had ever mentioned anything to us about Gus having a son.

"I think he would've turned, oh . . . twenty-one on Thursday? Twenty-two? Twenty-one, I think," Wilda said.

"Gus has a twenty-one-year-old son?" Sam gaped at her.

"No one mentions him anymore. Gus goes crazy if anyone talks about Jack. A year ago I asked Gus if he had any word from him, and Gus looked like he wanted to snap me in two. For a while after Jack ran off, there was lots of whispering about him, but now it's as if he never existed."

"What happened? Why did he run away?" Sam asked. Her voice was thin; I could tell she was reeling from the news, as I was. How could we have worked for Gus for over two months and not known this about him?

Wilda shook her head. "Well, I think it all goes back to his ex-wife and that whole mess."

"What exactly happened with her?" I asked. "Do you know the details?"

She looked wary. "You can't let Gus know I've been

telling you things about him, he'll never let me hear the end of it. But . . . you two spend more time with him than anyone else does . . . maybe you can figure out how to help him." She lowered her voice. "The truth is, Gus's wife left him for another man."

"Really?" Sam asked.

She nodded. She was about to tell us more when Alby called out for another order of bacon. She took care of him and the rest of her customers; when business slowed down, she came back to tell us the rest of the story.

"So who did Gus's wife leave him for?" I asked.

"She—Victoria—left Gus and Jack in Chicago and fled to Italy five years ago," Wilda said. "With a painter named Raul."

Raul? Visions of a lean, dark-haired, mustached man with a long brown cigarette floated through my head.

"Gus and Jack were completely devastated. I think that's when Gus started developing some of his, uh, bad habits. Drinking . . . you know."

We nodded. When we'd first met Gus he was splayed in our garbage with a huge wad of mayo in his ear. Our first project as his assistants had been to clean up his office, which had resembled a trash dump, with piles of clothes, books, papers, beer cans, and an ancient, broken Mr. Coffee maker strewn across the floor. It had finally taken shape, but now Gus himself looked like a disaster. He'd seemed so much more together in the last few months—until today.

"The Chicago PD wouldn't put up with his absences

anymore, so Gus switched to an office job with the force in Indy. But after a year he just kept getting worse. Finally they made him retire. He and Jack moved to Venice, and he decided to become a private detective."

Sam cocked her head. "How do you know this whole story? Gus never talks about himself at all."

Gus hated talking about his past, so we didn't ask him about it, and he never asked us about ours, either— a situation that worked well for all of us.

"Jack used to come in here a lot. He told me everything," Wilda said.

I propped my elbows on the table. "What was he like?"

She smiled. "Jack was the sweetest, smartest boy you could imagine. Always as polite as could be. That boy could eat four burgers and a plate of fries the size of my head and still have room for pie." To Wilda, a large appetite was emblematic of a big heart. "And he was brainy—he could recite any of Shakespeare's sonnets off the top of his head. He was the lead in all the musicals at Venice High for a couple years—*The Pajama Game, On the Town, West Side Story, Grease*—Jack was so talented. Just listening to him made quite a number of young ladies in Venice swoon." She grinned.

I tried to picture Jack dancing—I imagined a miniature Gus, burly, balding, and plump, prancing onstage in a tutu.

"What made him run away?" Sam asked.

"Well, no one's entirely certain what happened. But Gus and Jack had a huge blowout two days before Jack's graduation from Venice High. They never really got along so well—both were stubborn, hotheaded . . . but this fight was the worst they'd ever had."

"What was it about?" I asked.

"I'm not sure. Jack never told me the details. I think some of it had to do with the fact that Jack refused to go to college—he wanted to go to L.A. or New York and try to make it in show business instead. Gus said Jack should go to a regular college or the police academy just like Gus, his father, grandfather, and great-grandfather had. Jack refused. The day after his graduation three years ago, Jack left a note for his dad on the kitchen table and took off." She stared at a crumpled napkin. "No one has heard from him since."

As she told this story, some things about Gus began to make sense: the sadness I'd always sensed in him as he buried himself in his drinking; his reserve in talking about his family and his past; the noticeable lack of photos in his office and apartment. We'd thought he was just unsentimental, but maybe there was more to it. Maybe he was trying to forget something—or someone. I remembered a comment he'd made when we'd met his sister Rita in Chicago while we were working on our last case. He'd mentioned something about law enforcement being a legacy in the Jenkins family "until"—and then he'd paused and wouldn't say any more. He must have meant Jack.

"So where did Jack go?" Sam asked.

Wilda shrugged. "Who knows?"

I squinted at her. "Didn't Gus look for him? I mean he specializes in missing persons cases—"

"He looked," Wilda said. "Did he ever look. He

combed Indy, Chicago, L.A.. . . . he searched all over. It was all he did for a year or so. He came close to finding him a couple times, I heard. But I think Jack didn't want to be found."

She stared at the table. "Gus was at his lowest when you two girls came to Venice. I hope you girls know how much he's changed since you've started working with him. What a huge difference you've made. I mean he used to come in here and"—she started to whisper— "he looked so sketchy, some of my customers would change seats. He even . . . well, he didn't always smell so good, either."

"Lovely," Sam said.

"Gus needs to start looking for Jack again," she said. "I mean my daughter Rosa and I've had our tough times, but we never lost touch. She comes to visit when she can, and we talk on the phone. But as far as I know, Gus hasn't seen or heard from his son in three years. That's a crime, if you ask me."

I nodded. Alby yelled after her with yet another request. Wilda attended to him and her other customers, and a few minutes later Sam and I paid for our meals and said good-bye to Wilda. She handed us a Turkeyluck invite to give to our friend Colin, and reminded us not to tell Gus what she'd said.

Sam and I walked along the bare, dry canal bed that had given the town its name. We strolled past the stores that lined Main Street—It's Christmas!, which sold Christmas paraphernalia year round (I always wondered, who bought Christmas ornaments in July?), the thrift shop Second Hand Rose, and Bertha Kirk Intimates, which featured lingerie for larger ladies.

"I know what you're thinking," Sam said, "and the answer is no."

I stopped walking. "What am I thinking?"

We stood by the gazebo at the top of the street. She gave me a hard stare. "You know."

"Um . . . I'm thinking that hemlines are up this season? Earth tones are in?"

She smirked. "You think we should look for Jack. But there's no way. Gus would kill us if we started poking around in his past. He'd go berserk. I mean we wouldn't want him looking into our backgrounds." She hugged her elbows.

Of course I did think we should find Jack. "Well, we don't have to tell Gus what we're doing."

"How could we do it without him knowing?"

"If he keeps up with the way he's been acting, I doubt he'll be coming to the office all that much. We could look through the databases and the Internet, and I could ask around at school . . . we could just see if any information comes up," I said.

We walked past the gazebo and down our street. "Maybe Gus'll just get over it," Sam said. "In a few days he'll be back to his old self."

"Get over it? I don't think he's ever been over it—I mean it makes sense now why he's such a mess, doesn't it? His office, all those hours he spends at the bar . . . I mean, we've heard he was once one of the smartest guys on the force. Don't you think we should help him?"

She picked a Save the Canal flyer off the ground. "Why do you think we'd have any luck finding Jack? Gus didn't, and it sounds like he looked pretty hard."

"That was three years ago. We have updated databases and search engines now. It's ridiculous that Gus is so upset about all this, and yet his son is out there, waiting to be found and brought back to his dad. You heard what Wilda said—it's a crime."

Sam sighed. "We can't fix everything, Sophie."

"I'm not trying to fix everything. I just think we should fix this."

Three

We stopped by Colin's shop to give him the Turkeyluck invitation. Colin lived above a store he ran called Wright Bicycles, Etc., in a yellow Victorian house just a few blocks away from ours. The store had more "Etc." than bikes—he sold all sorts of tchotchkes ranging from gargoyles to antique farm equipment to early editions of poetry books by Edna St. Vincent Millay.

Colin was unpacking a crate of old board games—Life, Monopoly, Sorry—onto a table in the store. "Hey," he said when he saw us, and smiled. "What are you two up to on this fine Sunday evening?"

"Wilda asked us to give this to you." I handed him the invite.

He saw the turkey-shaped card and knew what it was. "Turkeyluck. My favorite holiday of the year."

"You've gone before?" Sam asked.

"Well, my dad's out of town so much, I've gone a couple of times." Colin's mother had died of breast cancer three years ago, and his dad was an international business lawyer who was nearly always traveling.

"What do you usually bring?" I asked.

He shook his head. "Last year was a disaster. I tried to bake bread but it came out weighing about fifty pounds. Henry broke a tooth on it. I thought he was going to sue me."

"Sophie knows how to make bread," Sam said.

I shrugged. I used to bake challah with our mom, but that was over six years ago.

"Maybe this year you can show me how. We've got to have some good bread to do justice to Gus's ubiquitous cheeseballs," he said with an eyebrow raised.

"Speaking of Gus . . . we just found out he has a *son*," Sam told him.

"Oh." Colin's lip twitched. His ears turned slightly red.

"You *knew*," I said. "You knew Gus had a son and you *didn't tell us?*"

"Well . . ." He looked embarrassed. "I'm sorry. But first off, I like my life—you know, being a living, breathing human being, without having to worry about an ex-cop trying to murder me. If Gus knew I'd told you, I'd be buried in the backyard right now. And also, well, I think it's important to respect people's privacy."

My stomach warmed a little at that—not that Colin knew who we really were, or that I could ever tell him, but at least if he had suspicions he'd probably keep them to himself.

"Also I never really knew Jack . . . I was still in middle school when he was at Venice High." Colin was a junior, a year ahead of me. He stared at the bookshelves. "You know, though, I think I have an old yearbook somewhere that might have him in it." He walked over to one of the many towering bookshelves in his shop and pulled out a dusty volume. *Venice High Cannoli 2000.*

"Cannoli? As in the pastry?" I asked.

"There was a vote over yearbook titles years ago and somehow *Cannoli* won. I don't think anyone had ever actually eaten one."

I thought of the Italian bakeries we'd stopped in on trips to Brooklyn when we were younger. I missed getting a good chocolate cannoli, and fresh mozzarella at a real Italian deli. I missed all the foods of our old neighborhood—spinach pies at the Turkiyem store on Forty-seventh street in Queens, and sweet rice-and-bean cakes at the Korean grocery. Not surprisingly, they didn't sell those at the Venice Kroger's.

Colin flipped through the dusty book until he reached Jack's page. "Here he is."

I wasn't prepared for what I saw when I looked at Jack's picture. He wasn't a miniature Gus. He wasn't miniature at all. In fact, he was a tall, muscular, larger-than-life certifiable hunkola. I couldn't believe what I was seeing.

"That's Jack?" My voice was hoarse with disbelief.

Colin squinted. "What?"

Sam stared at the page. "Wow. I guess he takes after his mom."

"What's the big deal?" Colin asked.

"He's *hot*," I said.

Colin rolled his eyes. "Oh, please. He's old enough to be your grandpa."

"Grandpa? He's twenty-one," I said.

Colin snapped the book shut. "Too old for you."

"He's right, that's way too old for you, Sophie," Sam said.

"I'm not saying he's 'for me,'" I said. "I just . . . I think he looks like a nice guy. I think Gus must have a very nice son."

Colin shook his head. "Here we go again. Troy, Pete . . . you pick the worst guys." He stuck the book on the table.

I was indignant. "I didn't pick anybody. I'm just commenting. Can't a girl comment?"

Sam picked up the yearbook. "*Anyway*. Sophie thinks we should find him." She told Colin how Gus had been acting lately, and about his downtrodden appearance at the diner.

"I don't know." Colin shrugged. "If Gus found out you were looking for Jack, you'd be in a lot of trouble. A couple years ago Officer Alby asked Gus about an old parking ticket Jack had never paid. Gus almost punched him."

"But Gus is so miserable now. It seems to me that since he and Jack are both *alive*, it's ridiculous that they're apart. If a member of your family is out there in the world, then everything possible should be done to find them."

Colin and Sam nodded. I wondered if they were thinking, as I was, about the people we'd lost. "Family," our dad used to say, "is the most important thing." During the brief period when I thought Josh and Leo were our relatives, I was so ecstatic at the thought of having some family again. The truth that they weren't related to us, that we had no relatives, was still unbearable. I thought that deep inside, Gus probably wanted to be reunited with Jack, but that desire had just become too deeply buried and forgotten.

"It sounds like you've made up your mind already,"

Colin said to me with his lopsided grin. "You're going to start searching for him no matter what."

"Well, I was thinking I'd poke around school a little," I admitted. "See if anyone has any leads. I'll be really subtle."

Sam looked through the board games on the table. She sighed. "All right, I guess I could do some subtle searching on my end, too. But if Gus gets the slightest suspicion of what we're up to, or if we don't find any leads, then we put it to rest. Agreed?"

"Agreed," I said.

I picked up the yearbook. "Can we borrow this?"

"Sure," Colin said. "Don't drool on it, though." There was a note of annoyance in his voice.

"I won't," I said drily.

Sam picked a decrepit orange box out of the stash of games. "Ooh—look at this."

"I found that at a yard sale this morning," Colin said. He was always combing yard sales looking for things to sell at his store. "I thought you'd like it."

Sam wiped about a half inch of dust off it. I stood next to her and read the box: *Big Boggle. Parker Brothers' Bigger Challenge 3-Minute Word Game. Fast-paced, no waiting, everyone plays at once.* "Like a new improved Scrabble," I said.

"I used to play with my dad ages ago, but I don't know what happened to the set we had," he said. "I haven't played it in years."

"Let's play now," Sam suggested.

I read the instructions inside the box. "Should we do it the conventional way, or the Lorna way?" We always played Lorna Scrabble, a version of the game our mom had made up. The only rule was that you had to make up fictional words from the letters you picked, then invent a plausible definition for each word; if you used a real word, you lost the game.

"Let's try the conventional way," Sam said.

We tried. In the first round Colin beat us both by twenty points. In the second round he beat us by over thirty, since he apparently knew every obscure word beginning with *qu: quag, quay, quean, quern, quod,* and *quorum.*

I'd been happy with my one *quinoa.*

Sam and I were dumbounded. "How is it possible that you know every single *qu* word in English?" Sam asked.

He blushed. "I think I memorized them when my dad and I used to play."

We nodded, impressed.

"You think I should go pro?" he asked.

"Definitely," I said. "You can start a Boggle team at Venice High."

"Nah—then I'd be a jock," he said.

We laughed. During the third round, I read my list. "I've got *murmur, murma,* and—"

"Wait a minute. *Murma? What's a murma?*" Sam asked.

"A mermaid mother of course," I said. "Duh."

"There's no such thing. We're not making up words here, Sophie. We decided."

"I didn't make it up. It's real."

Sam flipped through the dictionary. "It's not in here," she said with satisfaction.

"Well, that's obviously a crappy dictionary." I continued with the rest of my list. *"Wigs, wuv . . ."*

"Wuv?" Colin asked.

"Wuv," I said. "Of course. You know, as in, *I wuv you.*"

"Sophie, I'm touched," he said. "You wuv me?"

"I do," I said.

Sam shook her head. "Well, if you get *wuv,* then I'm getting points for *chéri.*"

"That's French," I said. "You can't use French."

"Then what's *wuv?* Speech-impedimentese? Also it's three letters and you have to have at least four letters in Big Boggle." She showed me the instructions to confirm this.

Sam and I bickered back and forth for a few moments until Colin said, "Now I see why the Lorna method was invented."

We finally decided to call it quits. We put the game away, hugged Colin good-bye, and walked home. I carried the yearbook.

"God, he's got the Boggle gift," Sam said, sincerely impressed.

"I know. That's why we wuv him. Do you wuv Josh?"

She sighed and tapped the yearbook in my arms. "You wuv Gus's son. That's weird."

"Well, he's hot. Could you believe that picture?" I flipped through the book and looked at it again under the streetlamp.

She tilted her head. "I hope that's not the reason you want to find him."

"Of course not. What kind of detective would I be if I only searched for handsome studmuffins?"

She laughed. "A happy one."

When we reached our porch, I paused for a minute. I heard a noise.

"What was that?" I asked Sam.

"What?"

"I heard—" I listened closely. *Mewww.*

I crouched down and looked under the porch. Two green eyes stared back. A second later a skinny, scraggly gray cat emerged. She rubbed against my ankles.

"She's so cute." I petted her and scratched her head.

"What are you doing?" Sam asked. "You're going to get rabies."

Along with many native New Yorkers I knew, Sam wasn't too fond of cats. She equated them with rats, mice, pigeons, and other stray city animals.

"Oh, come on, look. She's so sweet. She doesn't have a home. At least I don't think she does. She's not wearing a collar." The cat followed me up the steps to our porch.

"You're not bringing that thing in the house," Sam said.

"I don't think she has anywhere to go." The cat stuck her long neck out toward me, crouched down with her shoulder blades sticking out, and coughed. And coughed, and coughed. She was having a full-fledged coughing fit.

Sam stood back. "What's wrong with it? It sounds like Zayde." Before he died, our grandfather, Zayde, frequently produced dramatic, phlegmy, echoing coughs.

The cat kept coughing. I petted her again, hoping that would make her feel better, and she finally stopped.

"Poor little Zayde," Sam said to her. "I hope you don't have fleas."

"She doesn't have fleas." I scratched her behind her ears. "Don't listen to the mean lady," I told the cat.

Sam unlocked the door. "I'm going to give her something to eat," I said. "Stay there, kitty," I told the cat. "I'll be right back."

"Why are you talking to it? Do you think it understands English?"

I ignored her. "I hope we have some tuna."

"Don't tell me you're going to waste perfectly good tuna on Zayde."

I opened a can of tuna as Sam glared at me, and put it on the porch with a bowl of water.

"Just don't bring that thing in the house," Sam called out from the living room.

I petted the cat on the porch and watched her gulp down the entire can of tuna in about three seconds. The phone rang inside.

"Sophie—it's Mackenzie!" Sam called out.

I went inside and picked up the phone. Mackenzie and I had met my first day of school at Venice High, two months ago. We'd quickly become close friends. She loved to read everything from Jane Austen to *Cosmopolitan,* just like I did; we'd clicked right from the start. She lived on a farm fifteen miles outside of town with a cat, goats, pigs, chickens, and sheep.

"Hey—I just found the cutest stray cat," I told Mackenzie.

"What color is it?" she asked quickly.

"Gray," I said

"Oh." Her voice wavered.

"What's wrong? Are you okay?"

"I guess for a second I was hoping you'd found Yoda. I know that's ridiculous . . . you know what Yoda looks like. But she hasn't been home for three days now. I mean sometimes she'll go off and we don't see her for a couple days, but she's never been gone for this long before. I'm getting worried. I hope . . . I'm just afraid something's happened to her."

I pictured Yoda, Mackenzie's brown-and-black speckled calico cat, roaming around the farm. "She's probably just out hunting. Remember you told me Yoda caught that mole that time, which was like three times her size? She's probably out stalking a deer or something."

Mackenzie mustered a faint laugh. "I hope so. I guess I just need to stop worrying. My mom and I went out looking for her, but we couldn't find her anywhere."

"I'm sure she'll come back," I said.

"I hope you're right." We talked about homework for English class, and I told her about Gus's son. Since she was my age, six years younger than Jack, she'd never known him. Before we hung up she said, "Let me know if you happen to see any little calico cats on your way to school."

"I'll keep an eye out," I said.

The water was running in the upstairs bathroom; Sam must have been brushing her teeth. I ran outside and petted the cat. "I'm sorry I can't bring you inside," I told her. I petted her for a while longer and left her asleep in a little ball on our porch swing.

four

At school the next morning, Mackenzie was still upset about Yoda. "I couldn't sleep last night," she told me in English class. "I know it's sort of silly . . . she's just a cat. But I've had her since I was ten. She's a part of our family." She let out a little nervous laugh and shrugged.

"I know," I said, though I didn't really understand how she felt. I'd never had a pet I really loved. I used to plead with my parents to let me have a cat or dog, but my dad was allergic. After my relentless badgering, he'd finally agreed to let me have a hamster, Bob, who grew enormously obese. Sam renamed him Fatso. One day when I was eight, we decided to let Bob experience the fresh air of our Queens stoop (Sam's idea); he ran down the steps and into a manhole, never to be seen again. I told Mackenzie about Bob and his sad fate, changing the stoop to a lawn in Cleveland.

"You're not cheering me up," she said.

"Sorry. Yoda's much better equipped at surviving though. I'm sure she'll be okay."

Unfortunately my attempt at optimism was rendered useless later that afternoon. As Mackenzie and I joined the crowds swarming down the hall after our last class of the day, we bumped into Fern, who was trying to wriggle through the crowd as fast as she could. I'd first met

Fern at the Rose Country Club, where Sam and I'd gotten jobs over the summer; during the school year Fern worked in the administrative office at Venice High. She was about Wilda's age (which they both described as between thirty and fifty-five, though I was pretty sure it was closer to the fifty-five end), and her office was decorated with poodle-themed needlepoints.

Fern was nearly in tears. Her face was almost as red as her high-heeled shoes. She held a large piece of paper in her hands.

"Are you okay?" I asked her.

"The copier in my office is broken, and I need to get to the copy room. I've got to put these signs up."

"What's going on?" I asked.

She showed me the sign she was holding:

MISSING!

Name: Isabel Dingle
Color: Ecru
Height: 2 feet
Weight: 55 pounds
Distinguishing features: puffy fur at tail, puffy fur at ankles, floppy ears. Pink collar studded with rhinestones.

Isabel was last seen in the yard of 1427 Picadilly Lane in Venice. She is smart and affectionate and loves to eat chicken, hamburgers, flank steak, and macaroni and cheese. She likes to be brushed and to have her haunches massaged nightly. If found, please contact Fern Dingle at 555-8076.
Substantial reward!

Mackenzie froze. She told Fern about Yoda.

"I'm so sorry," Fern said, touching Mackenzie's arm. "Then you know what I'm going through."

"When did she disappear?" I asked.

"Every day I go home at lunchtime. Sometimes I find Izzy in the yard—I've got a doggy door—and today I went home, I called, 'Hi, Izzy, I'm home! Isabel, I got chicken! Izzy . . . Izzy?' and she was nowhere. I looked everywhere. She wasn't in the house. I opened a can of chicken—chicken always makes Izzy come running. But she didn't. I looked all over the yard, and for blocks around the neighborhood. She was gone." Fern swallowed.

"This is weird," Mackenzie said. "Do you think it's connected?"

Fern's eyes grew round. "You mean a pet thief?"

"It's probably just a coincidence," Mackenzie said. "Yoda's probably still off hunting, and maybe Isabel just got loose and ran away, or something."

"She'd never run off," Fern said. "She's never done that before."

"Why would someone take them?" I asked. "That'd be a really sick thing to do."

"I should make up some signs, too," Mackenzie said.

"You're welcome to come with me to the copy room. You can make your sign on the computer there and we can go around town and put them up together," Fern said.

Mackenzie nodded. "That sounds great."

"Do you want help?" I asked. I'd planned to spend

the afternoon visiting Mr. Moncrief, the drama teacher, to find out what he remembered about Jack Jenkins, but this seemed more important.

"We'll be fine," Mackenzie said. "We'll call you later with an update." She knew what I'd planned to do, but was careful not to say it in front of Fern, since I didn't want word about what I was doing to get around.

I wished them luck, hugged them good-bye, and headed to the drama room.

I'd never met Mr. Moncrief, although Colin had told me a few things about him. He said Moncrief had taught at Venice High for forty years, and talked in a British accent although apparently he'd never left the United States. He had long white hair and was rumored to be about 150 years old.

The drama room was on the top floor and set up like a mini-amphitheater, with ascending rows of seats. Students filed out; Mr. Moncrief stooped behind his desk and haphazardly stuffed loose papers into a tattered leather bag. His Rip Van Winkle–esque beard fell from his chin in scraggly waves; he accidentally caught a few strands in the zipper of his bag.

I waited till the last student had left the classroom and he'd extracted his beard from the zipper, then stepped in front of his desk. "Mr. Moncrief?"

He peered at me through Benjamin Franklin–style glasses. "Yes, my dear?"

"Um . . . I'm trying to find out some information about an old student of yours. Do you remember Jack Jenkins?"

His eyebrows raised. "Jenkins, yes. Of course I remember him. Haven't encountered a talent as big as that in years. A true thespian, if I ever saw one. Yes, Jack." He chuckled. "What can I tell you about him?"

"I'm trying to track him down, since he and his dad haven't been in touch in years . . . but I'd appreciate it if you don't mention this to anyone because, well, his dad doesn't know I'm doing it." I explained the whole situation to him.

"Of course, mums the word," Mr. Moncrief said. My eyes settled on the wall behind him. It was covered in theater posters:

WILSHIRE SUMMERSTOCK

Presents

THE FANTASTICKS

Starring
GERARD MONCRIEF

INDIANAPOLIS SHAKESPEARE OUTDOORS
Brings You

A Midsummer Night's Dream

Starring
GERARD MONCRIEF

He caught me staring at the *Midsummer Night's Dream* poster.

"I was Bottom," he said. "One of the great performances of my career, I believe." He gazed up at the ceiling and seemed to transcend into some sort of reverie. His voice burst out:

Methinks, mistress, you should have
little reason for that: and yet, to say the truth,
reason and love keep little company together
nowadays. The more the pity, that some
honest neighbors will not make them friends.

When he stopped, I wasn't sure what I was supposed to do. Clap? "That was great," I said feebly.

"Some think it's a lowly donkey, but scratch a donkey and you find brilliance, I always say."

I nodded. I wasn't sure if he was joking or not. "So have you heard from Jack since he ran away three years ago?"

He shook his head. "Not a peep. The boy evaporated like the mist on the moors, that he did."

"I know—I Googled him, but nothing came up that seemed related to him." The night before, when Sam and I'd looked for Jack on the Internet, over two thousand entries had come up, but it didn't seem like any of them were Gus's Jack. No actors, no one on Broadway as far as we could tell. Just some software developers, an army sergeant, and a chef, among lots of other professions.

"Pardon?" Mr. Moncrief asked.

"Googled? On the Internet?"

"Internet," he repeated.

He had heard of it, hadn't he? I was about to explain what it was when his features darkened. "Why do you waste your time on such poppycock? Crikey, girl! You should be outside frolicking in the grass! Youth is wasted on the young, I always say."

"Well, um, I frolic . . . I mean, I try to frolic when I can." I wanted to get on his good side so that he could reveal some information. I'd never had a teacher like him before. I had been a voice student at LaGuardia, my old school; I'd never taken a drama class, but I was pretty sure the drama teachers there were a little less eccentric than Mr. Moncrief. Colin had told me Moncrief had become an adjective in Venice: when referring to something melodramatic or theatrical, people called it *moncriefy*.

"So I thought maybe Jack might have gone to Los Angeles, to Hollywood or something, to pursue his career. Do you think he did?" I asked.

"Hollywood! Bloody Hollywood. The real theater is between you and me, man-to-man . . . do you think thespians in the Bard's time were allowed a hundred takes for one scene? One scene?! That's not acting! It's puppetry!"

"Oh. Okay," I said. "Well. Is there anything you remember about him that might help me?"

"There is one piece of advice I gave him that may prove useful to you. I always thought he'd have more luck if he changed the spelling of his name to Jacques.

Perhaps he took my advice. You might look under the name Jacques."

"Jacques Jenkins?"

"You could try that, although I myself recommended he work under the name Jacques Juneau. I thought it had a lovely ring to it. A fine, fine actor, yes indeed. I believed he'd go far. He had the gift."

"Really? What was he like?"

He held his hand upward. "Every audience was in the palm of his hand." He made a fist. "You can see for yourself. There should be videos of his performances, if you check the AV room."

"I will, I'll look for those. Thank you so much," I said. I left him my phone number in case he thought of anything else that might be helpful.

I was about to say good-bye when he asked me, "My dear girl, have you ever considered a career in theater?"

"Um—well, I like to sing, but I've never acted before."

He placed his fingertips under my chin and held my face up to the light, examining it. "Quite a youthful face, a little round, but so was Vivien Leigh's before she came of age. You might go far, my dear, if you put your mind to it."

"Thanks," I said.

I laughed to myself as I left the room, and in the hall I called one of Colin's friends, Fred Lamb, who was on the AV squad. He was already at home, but said he'd let me in to the video archive tomorrow to look for Jack's tapes.

I spent the rest of the afternoon and evening at home looking for Jacques Jenkins and Jacques Juneau on the Internet. I found a Jacques Jenkins involved with the National Ready Mixed Concrete Association—not our Jack. And there were many Jacques Juneaus, but most were French and none matched what I knew about our Jack Jenkins. I called a few Jacques Juneaus in Cocoa, Florida; Amelia, Ohio; and Tiverton, Rhode Island, but all were false leads.

Sam had left me a note that she was having dinner with Josh that night. At 9 P.M. I heard a car door shut. When she didn't come bounding in the house a minute later, I peeked out the window. My eyes bulged at what I saw.

In the dim light above our porch swing, Sam and Josh were entwined, kissing each other, limbs wrapped around everywhere like several spine-and-arm-twisting poses that my friend Viv and I did in a yoga class once. The kissing went on, the limbs wrapped, until finally I saw Sam's left eye open and stare right at me. I shut the curtain and ran back to my computer. A few minutes later the door opened.

"Sophie, were you spying on me?"

"Me? No. I've been at the computer the whole time." I smiled as innocently as I could.

"You were watching us kiss on the porch."

"Nope."

She gave me a look.

"That wasn't kissing—that was full-fledged making out!" I said.

She tried to act annoyed but couldn't. Her face was flushed and she was too happy. "Sophie—I really like him."

"I can tell." I wiggled my eyebrows, smiling.

She sighed.

"Hey, so what's the problem? This is good, right?" I asked.

"The problem is the same old same old—he has no idea who I really am and I'm afraid he's going to find out. Just the usual teenage run-of-the-mill problems. Do your *Seventeen*s tell you how to handle concealing your true identity?" she asked, pointing at my pile of magazines.

"No, I don't think they've covered that. It's a huge oversight in the teen magazine market."

"He just asks me so many questions, all about our time in Cleveland." Part of our story was that we'd come to Venice from Cleveland after a car accident killed our parents in June. We'd bought a whole bunch of Cleveland guidebooks—Tony Difriggio, our contact in the criminal underworld who lived in Indianapolis, even provided us with a photo of a house on a street where we'd supposedly lived with our parents. "He asks about our parents . . . it's just exhausting, lying all the time. No one ever told me that having a fake identity would be so tiring."

She shook her head and gazed off toward the porch. She'd left the front door ajar. A strange object seemed to be attached to the screen door.

We walked over to it. The stray cat from the night before was clinging to the screen with its claws, stuck on like a Halloween decoration.

We opened the screen, and the cat stayed stuck to it. Sam shut the door. The cat clung to the screen door, oblivious to it being opened and closed.

"Is she going to hang there all night?" Sam asked.

"I think she wants to come in," I said. "I think she's trying to send us a message."

I got her another bowl of water and a can of tuna. "Why can't we just let her sleep inside?"

The cat stared at us both plaintively through the screen, as if waiting for an answer. Sam was still considering this when the phone rang. It was Mackenzie.

"I'm at the Petal," she said. "I think you should come meet us here, right away."

"Why? What happened?"

"Um—Wilda wants to talk to you."

I heard muffled noises as the receiver changed hands, then Wilda's voice. It was crackly.

"Hi, Sophie?" Wilda asked. She didn't sound like herself at all.

"What's wrong?"

"Betty," Wilda said. "Betty's missing."

Five

Wilda sat slumped at the counter, her head down on top of her arms. Fern and Mackenzie perched on stools beside her. Wilda had closed the diner early; it was oddly empty and quiet.

"What happened?" I asked as Sam and I sat down at a table across from the counter.

"There's a pet thief on the loose," Fern said. "I'm sure of it."

Wilda let out a mournful sob. I suddenly wished I'd been able to convince Sam to let the stray cat inside our house, instead of leaving her on the porch.

"This afternoon, Betty was on the sidewalk in front of the diner sunning herself," Wilda said. "Just like she has a thousand afternoons before. I saw her there at four o'clock, then the diner got busy. I went back out there at six, and she was gone."

"Could she have wandered off?" Sam asked.

Wilda shook her head. "Sometimes she'll sashay down Main Street and go see Agnes Leary or one of the other shop owners. But she never goes farther than a couple storefronts. Never. Something's definitely happened to her."

"It's too much of a coincidence for all three to have

gone missing within days of each other," Mackenzie said.

"But why would someone steal two cats and a dog?" Sam asked.

"I've read about pet thieves in magazines," Fern said. "Just a few months ago *People* had an article about someone stealing cats in Colorado. They stole them and . . ." She hesitated. "They killed them brutally. The police thought it was a satanic cult or something."

All three of them turned a slight shade of green.

"I've heard about it, too," Wilda said. "There was a special on the news a few years ago about a whole industry of people who steal pets out of people's backyards and sell them to medical labs for research. They said something like a *million* pets are stolen each year. They sell them to puppy mills, pet stores, and dogfighting rings, too."

I tried not to picture Isabel in a dogfighting ring, with her well-groomed puffs.

"We talked to the police," Mackenzie said. "But it's bad news." She dug her hands in the pockets of her hooded sweatshirt. "Officer Alby was assigned to the case."

"Oh God," I said. "You might as well just look for the pets yourselves."

Wilda sighed. "We wanted Callowe to take on the case, but he said first off we need to wait seventy-two hours before they classify the pets as officially missing. Yoda's the only one who's been missing that long. Callowe seemed skeptical about there being a pet thief loose at all, but Alby believed us. Alby said he'd be willing to take on all three of our cases right away, before the seventy-two-hour waiting period."

It was somewhat comforting that the Venice Police Department would eagerly launch an investigation of pet thievery. But then again, the only other pressing crime was the toilet-papering of a few houses on Horse Chestnut Road on Halloween. I tried to imagine the NYPD jumping at the chance to look for missing cats and dogs.

"I thought Alby was downright kind about it," Fern said. She shrugged. "He might not be all that bad. I mean, he is trying to improve himself."

"Puh-leez," Wilda groaned. She rubbed her forehead. "He's been on that Atkins diet for weeks and hasn't lost an ounce yet. He couldn't find Isabel if she was in his own backyard. That's why we wanted to talk to you."

"Us?" Sam asked.

"We want you to convince Gus to take on the case," Wilda said.

Sam shook her head. "Ohhh no. Gus wouldn't take on a missing pet case in a thousand years."

"We trust him so much more than Alby," Mackenzie said. "We thought maybe if you two and Gus worked on it together, you'd find the pets in no time."

"You've seen Gus lately, though," I said. "He's not in the best shape, to say the least."

"I know," Wilda said. "But maybe it'd give him something to do, to get his mind focused."

It seemed doubtful to me that Gus would want to focus his mind on pets, but they were set on the idea.

"Maybe you can just bring it up to him and see what he says. You can show him these," Mackenzie said. She passed us copies of the flyers they'd made. They were photocopied on pink paper.

REWARD!

Name: Betty Higgins
Color: Black with white paws
Weight: 11 pounds
Disposition: Exceptionally sweet
Shape: Full-figured, with low-hanging belly

Betty was last seen on the sidewalk outside the Petal Diner on Main Street. She likes to have her tummy rubbed but does not like her tail touched. She likes to watch romantic comedies, especially those starring Hugh Grant. Distinctive melodious meow. Likes to sleep on top of heat vents. Please help find my beloved Betty! Large reward offered, in the form of food and/or cash. Contact Wilda Higgins at the Petal Diner, 555-1137.

LOST CAT! PLEASE HELP!

Name: Yoda
Color: Black-and-orange-speckled calico
Weight: 8 pounds

Yoda was last seen at Summerfield Farm on Rte 12. She is small, thin, and a successful and accomplished hunter. Will come when called by name. Has a white spot at the end of her tail. Loud purr. Anyone with information please contact Mackenzie Allen at 555-4101. Please help—we're heartsick!

Mackenzie had obviously taken the more concise approach. "Will you at least try asking him?" she said.

I nodded. "We'll try. If he doesn't want to do it, maybe Sam and I can help look for them on our own."

"That would be great," Mackenzie said. Wilda and Fern thanked us. They handed us an extra stack of flyers and a roll of tape so we could post the signs on trees and lampposts on our way home.

After Sam and I left the diner, she said, "He's not going to go for it. There's no way."

"Well, we can do it without him, I guess," I said, taping a Yoda flyer up to a maple tree.

"We have to let him know about it, though—we're already doing one case without his knowledge—two might be a little hard to get away with," she said. She stuck a Betty flyer on a lamppost. "He didn't show up to work today. He left a message that he was still feeling sick. I guess we can stop by his place tomorrow and tell him then—I want to check on him, anyway."

When we got back to our house, I was relieved to see that the stray cat was asleep on the porch swing. I scratched her head. She purred, then began another coughing fit.

"Poor Zayde," I said. I sat down on the swing next to her. "Maybe I should take her to the vet."

Sam nodded. When Zayde stopped coughing, she turned onto her back with her paws in the air, and Sam reluctantly scratched her belly. The cat purred and purred. I looked at Sam hopefully.

"All right, you can come in," Sam relented. She opened the front door, and Zayde trotted eagerly into our home.

The next day after school, we knocked on the door to Gus's apartment. He lived in the building adjacent to the Jenkins Detective Agency, two doors down from Muther's, his favorite bar. He didn't answer on the first try. After dozens of knocks and lots of shouts from us, we finally heard a "Whaaa?"

"Gus? It's us. Sam and Sophie."

"Mmmmph," a moan came from inside. "Grmmmph." We heard a few other grunts before he finally opened the door.

"We're sorry to bother you," Sam said. "But we wanted to see how you're doing."

"I'm fine," Gus said. He wore a white T-shirt splotched with a light brown coffee stain. He had pillow marks across his face, and the dark circles under his eyes looked even deeper than they had a couple days before.

"Look—we brought you soup—Wilda made it for you." I held up the pot.

"What kind is it?" he asked.

"Chicken noodle."

"Hmmmph." He peered under the lid. "Okay." He waved us inside.

His apartment was even more of a wreck than usual. The coffee table and couch were covered in newspapers, and the floor had massive heaps of laundry lumped around it. Mugs and glasses partially filled with various liquids were scattered around the floor and on the bookshelves. Empty beer cans overflowed from a cluster of paper bags in the corner. The TV was on but it wasn't getting reception; squiggly lines ran across the screen. Gus was walking strangely, too. His legs looked stiff and he grimaced as he sat down.

"You sure you're okay? You don't look so good," I said.

"Thanks." He yawned, baring his molars. "Everything all right at the office?"

"Everything's fine," Sam said.

I searched the kitchen for a clean bowl to serve the soup in. A huge tower of empty Swanson's Hungry-Man entrée boxes lay on the countertop. The sink was crammed with dirty dishes. I couldn't find a clean bowl, so I washed off a spoon and brought it to Gus with the soup pot. He seemed happier once he started eating.

I cleared the newspapers off a chair and sat down on it. "Actually—we've got a new case for you," I said, trying to sound especially excited and enthusiastic.

"Really?" He raised his eyebrows.

"Well, promise me you'll give it a chance before you dismiss it," I said.

"Yeah—just hear us out, and then we can talk about it," Sam said.

"Uh-oh." Gus looked suspicious. "What is it?"

"It's, um . . . some missing, uh, things around town," I said.

"Things? What things?" he asked.

"Um, *missingpets*," I mumbled quickly.

"Missing beds?" he asked. "Who'd steal beds?"

"Missing pets," I said. "Mackenzie's cat Yoda's missing, and Wilda's cat Betty, and Fern's poodle Isabel. They think there might be a pet thief in town."

Gus let out a full-fledged guffaw, his belly jiggling. "That's the funniest thing I've heard in weeks. No, what's the case, really?"

"That's it," Sam said. "They're really missing. Seriously."

The corners of his mouth turned down. "You're not kidding?"

We shook our heads.

He grumbled something unintelligible and stared at the pot of soup. He slurped up a spoonful. "Missing pets," he grunted. "This is what you got me out of bed for?"

"It's possible there really is a thief." I told him about the magazine article and TV show Wilda and Fern had described. "Alby took on the case, but of course no one trusts him to find them."

He closed his eyes and sighed. "This is ridiculous. Cats and dogs run off every day. Wait a week or so, I'm sure they'll turn up."

"What if they don't?" I asked.

"They can get some new ones." He slurped up another spoonful of soup.

"But they love their pets like people—they're not replaceable. Look." I showed him the flyers Wilda, Fern, and Mackenzie had made up; I thought they might prove to him how important the pets were to their owners.

"Pink paper. Nice touch." He read the flyers. "'Isabel Dingle'? 'Betty Higgins'? These animals have their owners' last names, too?"

I shrugged. "Well—"

"Oh, the poodle likes to have its haunches massaged every night, I see. Isn't that touching. And Wilda's cat likes Hugh Grant movies? Why am I not surprised?" He shook his head and handed the flyers back to me. "Let Alby do his job."

"Alby? Having Alby on the case is like having nobody at all. And if we don't do anything, the thief might strike again," I said, thinking about Zayde.

"Ohhh!" Gus cried with mock alarm. "The pet thief might strike again! Quick—lock the doors! I'm scared."

"It's business, though—a new case," Sam said. "They'll pay rewards," she added hopefully.

"Wilda and Fern aren't gonna cough up any cash for my services." He took a huge slurp. "And I don't work for soup."

"What if Sophie and I just look into it a little by ourselves, then?" Sam asked him. "As a favor to our friends?"

He let out a long sigh. "Don't tell me we're going to have a vote on this one, and you two will outvote me again." That's what we'd done when we decided to take on our last case.

"No—we won't do it without your approval," Sam said. She clearly wanted to appease him.

He fished the last noodle out of the pot. "You wouldn't put the Jenkins Agency name on anything? I don't want publicity for this."

"Of course not."

"Waste of your time, I think," he grunted, and gulped the last of the soup. A piece of noodle clung to his stubble. He peered in the pot, disappointed to see that it was all gone. "Who am I to tell you not to do it, though. Look at me." He shook his head and stared down at a little sliver of faded green carpet visible between the newspapers.

I felt like a force was pulling me downward; Gus was the lowest I'd ever seen him and I had no idea how to help, except for the long shot of finding Jack. Sam and I sat there quietly, not sure of what to say.

He gripped his knees. "I guess if that's all decided, then I'm going back to bed. Good luck finding Fluffy and Muffy and Puffy."

I didn't even have the heart to attempt to make some witty retort, as I normally would have. Instead we just told him we hoped he'd feel better soon, and to call us if he needed anything. Then we left the building and walked back to our car.

"I think he agreed to have us work on the pet case just to get us to leave him alone," Sam said.

I stared at the pavement. "He looks awful."

She opened the car door and climbed inside. "Maybe it will help, finding Jack." She whispered the name, even though there was no way Gus could hear us from the car. "Also, if he thinks you and I are focusing on the pet case, we can be using the resources in the office to simultaneously look for Jack, and he won't get suspicious."

I nodded. "I hope."

Six

When we got home, Sam made macaroni and cheese, and I popped the video of Venice High's 1999 production of *Grease* into the VCR. Fred had given it to me that afternoon during lunch, as well as a copy of Jack's 2000 *A Midsummer Night's Dream* performance. We sat on the couch eating our bowls of glutinous Day-Glo orange macaroni while we watched Jack onstage.

The quality of the tape was embarrassing. The camera had been mounted on a stationary tripod, so it only caught the action in the center of the stage; during part of the performance none of the actors were visible at all. When they did appear on tape they were often fuzzy and the colors were off. Jack played Danny Zuko, the male lead. Even with his skin appearing to be the same shade as our dinner, he was still handsome. His voice was pitch-perfect, and he danced with rhythm and force; his Danny Zuko gave John Travolta a run for his money.

"He's pretty good," Sam said, which was an especially high compliment coming from her, since she usually considered musicals a form of slow torture.

Moncrief was right: Jack had "it," that indescribable, magnetic thing that drew the audience in. I couldn't take my eyes off him. He was paired with an ill-matched costar (the girl who played Sandy was about a hundred pounds overweight, and you could see Jack strain as he lifted her in a dance scene), but he still made the show a success. Moncrief had added a few oddities to the musical: the characters launched into several original, poetic soliloquies. "I don't remember the T-Birds and Pink Ladies talking in iambic pentameter, do you?" Sam asked.

I shook my head, but Jack even made those scenes seem funny and natural.

Unfortunately the second half of the video was blocked by someone in a puffy down coat who decided to stand directly in front of the camera. We ejected that tape and put in *A Midsummer Night's Dream.*

Jack seemed more in his element in this play. He was Oberon, King of the Fairies. The best part was his costume, a skintight ethereal bodysuit that showed every rippling muscle.

I took out a sheet of paper and started making a list of notes about Jack.

"What are you writing?" Sam asked.

"Case notes," I said.

She peered over my shoulder. "Case number four-million-something? Have we had several million cases I haven't known about? I thought we were on our third one."

"I want it to look official."

"'Build: hard-bodied? Eyes: green and smoldering'?" Sam said, reading as I wrote.

"Just telling the truth," I said. She laughed.

Toward the middle of the play, there was a knock on the door. Sam got up to open it. It was Colin.

"Thought I'd see what you guys were up to tonight," he said. He glanced at the screen. "What are you watching? Public access?"

"We're having a Jack Jenkins retrospective," Sam said. She showed him the video boxes. "He's good."

Colin sat down beside us on the couch. "What's he wearing, a unitard? Why does he have a Tina Turner wig on?"

"He's Oberon," I said. I'd hardly noticed the wig; I'd been so distracted by his muscles.

They must have gotten a new cameraman for this production, because the angle swiveled to keep the actors in sight, and at one point it even zoomed to show Jack up close. Sam squinted and walked over to the TV set. "Good God, are those his *abs?*" she asked, tapping the screen.

"Yup," I said, smiling.

Colin shook his head. "I don't believe you guys."

Despite Colin's annoyance, Sam and I continued to gape at Jack's body until Zayde emerged from under the couch. So far, she'd spent most of her time in the house hiding under beds and various pieces of furniture. A surge of bravery must have suddenly engulfed her, however, since she hopped onto the couch and curled into Colin's lap.

"Is this the stray you told me about?" Colin asked.

"Yup—meet Zayde. Zayde, this is Colin," I said.

"Nice to meet you," he told the cat, and petted her. "Where'd you get the name?"

"Oh, you know." I tried to think of a way to explain why we named our cat the Yiddish word for "grandfather," considering we were supposedly Christian girls from Cleveland. "You know the writer Zadie Smith?" I asked.

He nodded. "I've heard of her. That's a good name." I sank back into the couch, relieved. He scratched Zayde's head. The cat rolled onto her back and stared up at him.

"She likes you," I said.

"What a flirt," Sam said. "Our cat has a crush on Colin."

But the romance was short-lived. Zayde turned over, jumped on to the coffee table, and began another coughing fit.

"What's wrong with her?" Colin asked.

I shrugged and smoothed her fur. "I don't know. We'll find out tomorrow. I made an appointment at the vet."

"Dr. Ergaster?" Colin asked.

I nodded. "You've heard of him?"

"Yeah. He's the only vet in the county, I think."

"That's what Mackenzie and Wilda said. They said he's great, and he runs a shelter, too. I thought I could ask him about the missing pets at the same time."

"What time's the appointment?" Sam asked.

"Four o'clock."

Sam wrinkled her nose. "Can you change it to later? I have two phone interviews scheduled for three and four tomorrow with people at Actors' Equity and the Screen Actors' Guild—I was hoping they might have some information on Jack, if he's had any acting jobs at all in the past three years," she said.

"I can take you if you need a ride," Colin offered.

"Really?" I asked. "You sure?"

"Of course. Anything for Zayde." He reached to pet her, but as soon as she finished coughing, she hopped off the coffee table and scrambled under an armchair. A piece of paper fell off the table and Colin picked it up.

"What's this?" he asked.

"Nothing." It was my case notes on Jack. I tried to grab it from him, but he held it away from me, out of my reach.

His eyes scanned the page. "'General description: Babelicious'? 'Hot hot hot'?"

"Well." I shrugged, embarrassed. I hadn't meant for him to read it.

"You're obsessed with the guy," he said.

"It's an important case," I said. "That's all."

Colin sighed. The phone rang and Sam answered it; it was Josh. She took the phone upstairs to her room to talk to him in private. Colin and I watched the video in silence, until a few minutes later Sam came halfway down the stairs and called out to us, "Hey, what are you guys doing Saturday night? Leo's klezmer band is playing at Wilshire College and Josh wants to know if you two want to come."

I'd forgotten that Josh still thought Colin and I were a couple. During our last case, Colin and I had to pretend we were together in order to accompany Sam and Josh on their first date.

"Sure," Colin called to her. "What's klezmer?" he asked me.

"I don't know," I said. "Sam, what's klezmer?" I yelled up the stairs, but she was already back in her room and didn't answer. I shrugged, as if I didn't know. "Beats me," I said.

He gazed upward. "I think I've heard of it actually—it's Jewish music, right? Like *Fiddler on the Roof*, kind of?"

"I don't know." My tone sounded defensive, but I didn't know what else to say. I had to get better at concealing these things. I stared intently at the TV, hoping he wouldn't ask me anything else about it.

He must have taken my tone as standoffish, since he said, "I guess I should just leave you to your drooling." He sounded half-joking and half-cold.

"I'm not drooling," I said.

"I'll see you tomorrow. Do you want to go right after school? I think it's about a half-hour drive over there."

"Okay. Thanks," I said, trying to sound normal again. "I really appreciate it."

He waved good-bye and let himself out. I lay sprawled on the couch, my head on the pillow, and stared at the screen. Watching Jack's plays had made me think about my own dreams. My old high school had launched so many people into successful careers in the performing arts—the whole movie *Fame* had been based on my school. I wondered if it was possible to go to high school in Venice and still have a successful career in music. In the back of my mind I'd always hoped I could have a career as a singer someday. I admired Jack for going after his dreams and trying to make it big. He was certainly talented enough to do it.

At the end of the play, Oberon leaned toward Titania.

I felt a small, surprising swell of jealousy as I watched them kiss.

The next day after school, Colin gave me a ride to the pet store so I could buy a cat carrier to take Zayde to the vet in. It was around the corner from Video Paradise, where our friend Fred worked on nights and weekends, but it had no sign announcing what it was. The front window was strung with blinking chili pepper lights, and the cash register was covered with postcards from all over the country—Hollywood, Sedona, San Francisco, Las Vegas. The young guy behind the register had his feet propped up on the counter while he read Jack Kerouac's *On the Road*. I picked out a carrier while Colin waited in the car—we were running late.

I had to ring the bell on the counter before the guy would even look at me. "Hello!" I said. "Can I pay for this carrier, please?"

"Hold your horses," he said. He put down his book. "Jeez. What's the rush?"

Sometimes I couldn't keep my impatient New York side from getting aggravated by the slow pace in Venice. "I'm late for a vet appointment," I said.

He had long black hair cut in a mullet, and multiple ear piercings. He looked for a price on the carrier, and when he didn't find one, he searched the shelf it came from until he finally said, "Eh, I'll just charge you fifteen for that." He wrote out a receipt by hand on paper that said THE STINKY ROSE PET SHOPPE.

"The Stinky Rose?" I asked.

He grinned. "I inherited the store from my uncle, and it used to be called the Rose Pet Shoppe. I renamed it. Thought it would shake things up around here a little. And it did—man, did it piss the Rose Society off. Bea Sellers, the president? She must've called me a hundred times, and shoved petitions at me . . . she wanted an ordinance on the books that all shops in Venice have *complimentary* rose references. I said, I just want my free speech. I won the battle, of course—though they made me take the sign off the store. But I get to keep it in my ads."

I smiled. "It's pretty funny."

"I also thought of it as sort of a metaphor. You know—pets can be stinky but sweet at the same time."

"Good point." I nodded toward *On the Road*. "That's a great book, by the way."

"You read it?" He held it up and looked at the cover.

"I loved it." I paid for the carrier, thanked him, and ran out the door.

"Good luck at the vet," he called after me.

It had taken twenty minutes to get Zayde into the cat carrier; I inspected the scratches on my arms, a result of the process, while she yowled during the drive. It was almost four-thirty when we finally arrived at the animal hospital. The sign on Meads Hollow Road had a picture of a cat, dog, and horse on it. The sign read:

Dr. H. Ergaster
Meads Hollow Animal Hospital and Refuge

The receptionist wore a lab coat printed with multi-colored cats. As we waited to be seen, I leafed through a binder filled with pictures of Dr. Ergaster's recent patients: a bunny with a massive abscess on its neck; a poor dog that had had a run-in with a porcupine. In the picture the dog looked like it was having acupuncture on its face. *We spent three hours picking quills out of Hortense's nose,* someone had written under the photo. *But afterward she was good as new!*

Ten minutes later, the receptionist led us in to see Dr. Ergaster. He was a small, wiry man, completely bald, with thick silvery eyebrows and owl-like brown eyes. We introduced ourselves.

"And who do we have here?" he asked.

"Zayde," I said. He opened the door to the carrier, but despite the fight she had put up going into it, now she didn't want to come out. Finally, he coaxed her onto the examining table. He weighed her, listened to her heart with a stethoscope, and administered her feline leukemia and feline AIDS tests. I moved closer to Colin as we waited for the results. I was surprised at how nervous I was. He put his hand on my shoulder.

"I hope she's okay," I said.

"Me, too." He sounded a little nervous also. I told him about my old hamster, Bob, and his tragic fate. "I didn't cry over him or anything, though," I said. "I've never felt worried about an animal before."

In a few minutes Dr. Ergaster gave us the results. "The tests are all negative," he said.

"Thank God." I smiled at Colin.

We told him about Zayde's coughing, and after listening to her breathing and taking an X ray, he diagnosed it as asthma. He gave her a shot of a corticosteroid, and said that like human asthma, there wasn't a cure for it, but hopefully the coughing fits would subside. He told us that keeping the house free of dust, mold, and fireplace smoke would help.

Before we left, I said, "I've got another question for you." I told him about the missing pets.

He nodded, his bald head shining under the fluorescent light. "I've gotten a couple calls about that. I know Yoda, Betty, and Isabel well. Unfortunately they haven't turned up here at the shelter yet."

"Do you think there could be a thief around town?" I asked him.

He pursed his lips. "Wilda and Fern told me about the articles they've read about pet thieves," he said, his hand gently holding Zayde in place on the examining table. "I don't know how a stranger could do that in a small town and escape unnoticed. If it is a thief, then it's someone in town, I think."

"Who would do that?" I asked.

He shook his head. "I wish I knew."

"Will you call us if you hear anything, or notice anything or anybody unusual?" I asked him.

"I will." He patted Zayde and loaded her back into the carrier with a lot more grace than I had.

Colin dropped Zayde and me back at home, and I thanked him for coming with us. When I went inside the house, the answering machine was blinking. The message was from Fern: "Girls, I found something in my yard . . . could you two come by my office tonight so I can tell you about it? I'm working late." I called Sam at work; she picked me up soon after and we drove over to see Fern.

"How did the phone interviews go?" I asked Sam in the car.

She shook her head. "Actors' Equity and SAG have no record of Jack at all. We searched under name—both Jack and Jacques—and date of birth, and Social Security number, but nothing came up. I've gone through all the databases Gus has, but there's no trace of him."

Fern was waiting for us in her office at Venice High, rearranging stacks of paper, sharpening pencils, and checking that all her pens still worked. Framed needlepoints proclaiming I LOVE MY POODLE and HOME IS WHERE YOUR POODLE IS hung from her wall.

"Yup, I'm still here," she said, tapping her fingers on her desk. "I can't help but work late since Isabel disappeared. I hate to go home to an empty house. It's not the same there anymore. She was—is—such a special dog. I never said that I owned her. She owned me. She owned me." She repeated the phrase the same way Tom Cruise repeated "You complete me" in *Jerry Maguire*.

"You said you found something in the yard?" Sam asked her.

She nodded. "My only consolation is that I know Isabel put up a fight. She was a lady but she would not go gently into the good night. No sirree. She was a fighter. A spark plug. Kind of like her mommy." She mustered a feeble smile.

"How do you know she put up a fight?" I asked.

She leaned toward us. "This afternoon I forced my-self to go home for a little while. I was poking around the yard, doing a little gardening, hoping to distract myself. I bent over my azalea bush—Isabel loved that bush—and I found a scrap of pale blue fabric, like from a men's button-down shirt, caught in the leaves. It was all torn and frayed at the edges."

Sam scribbled this down in her notepad. "Where is it?"

"Well, I went over to the Petal to tell Wilda, and Officer Alby was there. I showed it to him and he asked me to give it to him. He said it was important evidence."

Sam rolled her eyes. "Oh God, Alby. He's probably lost it by now, or touched it so many times it can't be an-alyzed."

Fern looked alarmed. "Do you think so?"

"I hope not," I said.

"I also talked to my next door neighbor, Sherman Frum." She made a face. "He was smiling at me over the fence that separates our yards. He said he's been sleep-ing better than he has in years now that Isabel's gone. I wonder if he did it. He always complained about Isabel's alleged 'barking.' She didn't really bark—she was just chatty, that's all. I think you should look into him."

"We will," Sam said.

We offered her a ride home with us, but she said, "I think I'll just stay here a little longer," and smiled wanly.

In the car, Sam glanced at her watch. "Josh said he

was going to stop by our house at 8 P.M.—he wants me to read over his economics paper for him."

"Economics paper, eh? I've heard that one before." I smirked.

"What are you talking about?" She squinted at me.

"'Economics paper' sounds like a euphemism."

"For what?"

"Gettin' busy." I wiggled my eyebrows.

"Oh, please." She turned onto our block. A horse-drawn carriage was parked a few feet from our house. "What's that?"

Chester, my mechanics teacher, who also owned the town garage, was in the driver's seat. We pulled into our driveway and Josh stepped down from the carriage.

"Hi." He kissed my sister on the lips.

"What's going on?" Sam asked.

"I got to Venice early and ran into Chester with this carriage on Main Street," Josh said. I thought it might be fun to take a ride."

"Where'd you get the horse and carriage?" I asked Chester. I petted the horse on its nose.

"I borrowed the horse from the Gallaghers' farm. I haven't used the carriage since the Rose Festival in 2000—it needed some repairs—but Alby asked me to do it. I had just dropped him and Agnes off at her house when I ran into your friend here. He asked me if it was for hire."

"Are you up for it?" Josh asked Sam. She nodded. "Do you want to come, too?" he asked me.

"No thanks," I said, knowing they didn't sincerely

want me on their romantic excursion. I pinched Sam. "Have fun working on the economics paper," I whispered, and watched them trot off.

I heard the clucking of horse hooves when Chester dropped Sam and Josh off. I met them downstairs. "How was it?" I asked.

Sam's cheeks were flushed. "I'll give it to Alby—he had a good idea. Chester's thinking of turning carriage rides into a regular business."

"How's Leo?" I asked Josh.

"He's really excited that you're coming for klezmer. He said he misses seeing you two."

"Really?" I bounced on my heels. I missed seeing Leo also. Even if he wasn't our relative, there were things about him that reminded me of our father and grandfather—his faint Yiddish intonations, his stories of life in Europe before the war, his warmth and sense of humor.

"He loves you guys," Josh said.

I grinned. "I'll, uh, let you two get to work on your paper." I went up to my room to do homework. I'd only completed a page of math when I heard a car pull up in the driveway. I looked out the window and saw Colin and Fred walking up the steps to our porch. I ran down to the living room.

Fred and Colin sat on the couch beside Josh. Fred's ears were red and he kept fiddling with his hands.

"Herman's gone," Fred said in a panicked voice. Herman was Fred's amiable, aging Labrador retriever.

Sam's mouth dropped open. "What happened?"

"When I came home after school, he was missing. My parents were still at work. I called my dad and he said he'd walked Herman when he was home for lunch like he always does, and everything seemed fine then. So he must've been taken between one P.M. when my dad went back to work, and three-thirty when I got home from school."

"This is crazy," I said. "I can't believe it."

"I combed through my neighbors' yards all after-noon, until the sun went down." He reached into his pocket and pulled out a red band with a little black box attached to it. "I found this—Herman's electric dog col-lar. It was in the Plattes' backyard, a few hundred feet away. It's never fallen off. You need a human hand to get that thing off Herman. Whoever stole my dog's got a good throwing arm, I'll tell you that much."

He ran his fingers through his bright red hair. "I should've been more careful. I shouldn't have let Herman run in the yard unsupervised. I mean . . . I guess I just didn't really believe this whole pet thief theory." He stood up. "I feel just awful."

"You didn't do anything wrong," Colin said. "Honestly, the whole idea of a pet thief seemed kind of ridiculous to me, too. I mean Herman was, um—no of-fense Fred—but what would someone want with a twelve-year-old Labrador?"

"He still acted like a puppy," Fred said indignantly. "I can think of a lot of reasons why someone might steal him."

"Colin has a point," I said. "This whole thing doesn't make sense. Dr. Ergaster said he thought if there was a thief, then it's probably an inside job—someone in town. Maybe someone we know."

"But who in Venice would want these pets?" Sam asked.

"What would their motive be?" Josh asked.

We stared at one another, none of us able to come up with an answer.

Seven

Before I fell asleep that night, I picked up the *Venice High Cannoli 2000* yearbook from my night table and leafed through it. I'd marked the three pages Jack was on with Post-its—page 110, his senior photo, taken sitting on the edge of the Venice High theater stage in jeans and a black T-shirt; page 46, a picture of him as Oberon on the drama club page; and page 27, a candid photo of him on the school lawn with a friend. I stared at him smiling in the grass. My gaze shifted to the guy sitting next to him. I'd hardly noticed him before, with his long black hair and his face shaded by the sun. I squinted at the picture.

It was the pet-shop guy.

I had my first lead. As soon as I saw Mackenzie in English class the next morning, I told her, "You know the guy who owns the Stinky Rose?"

"Wayne Westlake?" she asked. "With the mullet?"

I nodded. "He used to be friends with Jack." I told her about the yearbook photo. "I want to go talk to him today after school and see if he knows anything about where Jack might be. At the same time I can ask if he's noticed anything suspicious among his customers, for the pet case. Sam's spending the day going through files—will you come to the pet store with me?"

"Sure, sounds like a good idea." She paused. "I shopped there for Yoda." Her voice wilted.

I didn't know what to say. I'd never really understood how attached people could become to their pets before, but in the short time we'd had Zayde, I'd already begun to adore her: she had her hours under the couch, but she also greeted Sam and me when we came home in the afternoons, waiting at the door like a puppy; she curled herself into a ball and slept next to my stomach at night, and in the mornings she stretched out in the sunlight by my head, purring loudly. I thought about how much Mackenzie must miss her cat, and I let out a silent plea that we would find Yoda. Mackenzie had been so out of it for the whole week since Yoda had disappeared. We had to find her.

After school, Mackenzie and I rode in her truck to the pet store. The bells on the door rang as we entered. Today Wayne wore an ELVIS IS ALIVE AND I SAW HIM IN VENICE, INDIANA T-shirt, which was also for sale in the shop for the bargain price of $4.99. Aretha Franklin's "Respect" blasted from the radio. He was still buried in *On the Road*, his feet propped next to the postcard-covered cash register.

"Hi," I said, standing before him at the counter.

"Hello there," Wayne said, not taking his eyes off his book.

"Hey, Wayne," Mackenzie said.

He gave her a sidelong glance. "Any sign of Yoda?"

She shook her head and gazed at the floor.

"She'll turn up. Don't worry." He placed his book on the counter. "Cats have an extraordinary homing instinct. I saw a show on PBS about it once. There was a cat in England named Sooty who found his way back home from over a hundred miles away. And one named Tigger who made the trip back to his old home more than seventy-five times—on three legs."

"I guess that's sort of comforting," Mackenzie said, not looking that comforted. "Have you noticed anything strange at this place lately? Any suspicious activity? Any new customers buying supplies of food?"

"Nope, nothing at all." He fiddled with the earring dangling from his right ear. "Personally, I don't believe this thief theory. I think it's just a plot cooked up by Bea Sellers at the Rose Society to get publicity for some new festival or pet parade she's planning, once the pets turn up."

"I wish that's what it was," Mackenzie said.

"I haven't noticed any change at this place at all. Same old customers. No one new, except you," he said to me. "But not everyone in town shops here. We've got some sellouts who drive all the way to Indy to the Corporate Evil Pet Store Which Will Steal Your Pet's Soul to save a buck or two. Inferior food and inferior service. Is that what their pet's worth to them?" He shook his head.

The Aretha Franklin song ended and Wayne turned to a shelf behind him filled with vinyl records. "I sell these on the side as a hobby. You interested? I got a '79 Led Zeppelin *In Through the Out Door* and a '76 Steely Dan *Royal Scam*. Zep's unscratched. Steely Dan's still in the shrink-wrap. Mint."

"Uh, no thanks," I said. I wondered if he and Jack hung around listening to vinyl records. I tried to picture him and Jack as friends. What was Jack like, really?

"So . . ." I hesitated, trying to sound casual. "When did you graduate Venice High?"

"Two thousand," he said.

"Did you know Jack Jenkins?"

He looked at me slyly. "Why do you want to know?"

"I'm studying acting with Moncrief and he told me I should get in touch with Jack. He thought contacting someone in the field—someone as talented as Jack— would be really helpful." This was the lie I'd come up with while daydreaming in math class that day.

He leaned across the counter. "We're not in touch." He smiled. He was not a gifted liar; there was something coy about his tone, and I could tell he wasn't telling the truth.

"Do you know where he is?"

Wayne squinted at me, sizing me up, trying to tell if I was lying or not. He seemed unsure. Then he said, "I don't think so."

Don't *think* so? He was definitely holding something back.

He saw the look on my face and shrugged. "I can tell you that right after he left Venice, he went to Chicago for a little while. He got a job at a restaurant and was trying to save enough to go see his mom in Italy. I don't think he ever got enough together, though. He only worked part-time because he was going to auditions and doing some acting. Small stuff, like improv gigs, a couple local plays, summer stock. Maybe he did go to Italy, though. Who knows? J.J. always joked about becoming a real Venetian." He smiled his wily grin.

"J.J.?" I asked. "That's what people called Jack?" No one else had mentioned that. "Is that the name he's been going under?" I asked.

He shrugged again. "Moncrief wanted Jack to go French." He laughed. "But I don't think he did."

"So you think he's in Venice, Italy?" Mackenzie asked. "That's pretty exciting. Do you have any old addresses for him or anything?"

He shook his head. "Nope." He adjusted the Meowie Wowie catnip display on the counter.

It didn't seem like he was going to tell us anything else. "Well, let us know if you hear anything from Jack, or notice any suspicious pet-related activity," I said.

"Will do."

I bought a pouch of the Meowie Wowie for Zayde, we thanked him, and he returned to his book. Mackenzie and I walked back to her car.

"I don't think he was telling us the whole truth. I got the feeling he knows where Jack is," I said.

"Me, too," she said. "But I don't know how we can get the info out of him."

I'd called Fern's complaining neighbor, Sherman Frum, the night before and made plans to talk to him that afternoon as well. Mackenzie said she'd like to come, too, and we drove there straight from Wayne's.

Sherman Frum was a clockmaker; he had a small

business he ran out of his home. The house was filled with clocks from floor to ceiling, with bells and gongs going off at random intervals. Some clocks were transparent, so you could see all the gears working. The place was immaculate, with white carpeting and white walls, as was his clothing: a spotless white oxford shirt and pressed brown trousers.

"You said on the phone you were concerned about Ms. Dingle's animal?" he said in a scratchy voice as he led us down his front hall and into the living room.

"That's right," I said. "We just wanted to ask you a few questions about Isabel."

We sat on white sofas. "I have to tell you, I don't miss that pup at all," he said. "All that barking. I don't know why people let animals into their homes. Filthy creatures. And that dog had psychological problems—she didn't like men for some reason. That mutt would take one look at me in the yard and yap her head off. The only way I could get her to pipe down was if I gave her some meat. I tried that a few times, but I'd be a poor man if I spent all my money on fresh meat for the neighbor's overzealous poodle."

"What about the day she disappeared—Monday, November tenth? Did you hear the barking start or stop at a specific time?" I asked.

"I keep earplugs on all day while I work, but I can still hear that dog's yapper. That day in question I heard the usual woofing in the yard. Then it went quiet. It was eleven forty-one A.M.—I was working on a clock at the time. I was plumb glad for the sudden silence. I thought

Ms. Dingle must have taken the dog to the vet or some-thing. I didn't go outside, I didn't ask questions—I went straight to my nap. It was the best nap I've had in years."

"You didn't check outside or see anything?" I asked.

He shook his head. "That dog so much as sees me through the window, she goes bonkers. I didn't chance a peek."

We asked him a few more questions, but he didn't have any more information. We thanked him and walked down his steps, clocks chiming and cuckooing as he shut the door behind us.

"He's definitely not fond of animals," I said. "He has a motive, at least for Isabel."

"True," she said. "But he's certainly not harboring any animals on that spotless carpet."

"Yeah, and he seems too meticulous to have dis-posed of her—much too messy."

She grimaced. "Sophie. Yuck."

"Sorry."

Every tree we passed on the block displayed an Isabel flyer. "How's Zayde?" Mackenzie asked.

"She's good. We're not letting her out at all. I think she misses being outside, though—she keeps pressing herself up against the windows and scratching at them."

"Maybe you can get her to help find the culprit, like in those *Cat Who* mysteries." She smiled. "Those books about those cats who help solve crimes?"

"The only way Zayde's going to find anything is if it's right next to her food dish," I said.

* * *

We went to the Petal for dinner—we called Sam and asked her to join us, but she said she was in the middle of digging through Gus's files, looking for Jack info, and she wanted to finish up; she'd meet us later. She also had to delete all evidence of every database search she did so Gus wouldn't find out what she'd been doing if he came in the office.

We ran into Wilda in front of the diner, tying yellow ribbons onto the trees lining Main Street.

"I'm glad you girls are here. I wanted to let you know I'm hosting a Bring Our Pets Home candlelight vigil at the gazebo Sunday night. I hope you can make it."

"Of course," Mackenzie said.

"How are you doing?" I asked her.

She sighed. "All right, I guess. It's the guilt that's getting to me. Why did I let her sit outside of the diner—I shouldn't have let her do that. I shouldn't have let her parade around where everyone could see her. She was just too pretty for that. Of course someone would snatch her."

"It's not your fault," I said.

"That's what Alby told me. I didn't believe him, either. He's in the diner right now. He says he's made some progress but he didn't say what."

"Really?" I asked.

She nodded. "I'm almost done here. I'll come inside with you in a sec." She tied ribbons around a few more trees, and we walked into the diner. Alby sat in a booth, chowing down on a massive ground beef patty.

"He ordered a hamburger with no bun, no veggies,

nothing on it whatsoever—not even ketchup. He's killing me with this diet. He can't expect a culinary artist to express herself in protein only," Wilda said.

We sat at the counter and watched Alby consume his mound of meat. He was reading *Mars and Venus on a Date*. His copy of *Creating Respect* lay dog-eared and ravaged on the table, facedown.

"Maybe we can get him to tell us what this 'progress' is," Mackenzie said. "Let's ask him."

We walked over to his booth. "Hi? Um—Officer Alby?" Mackenzie asked.

He put down *Mars and Venus on a Date* and picked up a package of beef jerky off the table. "Jerky?" he offered. "It's hickory-smoked."

"Um, no thanks," we said.

"We just were wondering if you've had any developments in the case," Mackenzie said.

He smiled. "As a matter of fact, I have. I'm supremely confident I'll locate your cat Yoda and all the other unfortunate animals and return them to their rightful owners."

What were these books telling him? He sounded like he was being programmed by a computer.

"Fern said she gave you that piece of blue cloth she found in her yard," I said.

"It's at the lab right now being analyzed," he said. He leaned back in his booth. "Pet detection is a very involved, scientific process. But I'm supremely confident I'll solve this case shortly. I've got a prime suspect already."

"Who?" Mackenzie asked. "Sherman Frum?"

"Frum?" He wrinkled his nose. "No, no. The identity of the suspect is classified information." He tore off a piece of jerky and chewed it with his mouth open. "But it happens to be someone you know well."

"What?" I asked. "Who is it?"

He swallowed. "I'm not at liberty to say. But the suspect made a direct threat to Wilda about her cat last Sunday, in this very place."

I scrolled back in my mind, trying to figure out what he was talking about.

"He said Betty needed to be *gotten rid of*," Alby said.

I remembered. "Gus? Are you talking about *Gus*?"

He flinched with surprise that I'd guessed it right. "As I said, I'm not at liberty to—"

"He didn't mean it like *that*," I said, incredulous.

Alby raised his eyebrows. "That's for the law to decide." His eyes moved to the door just as Agnes Leary appeared at the threshold. "Now if you'll excuse me, I have a lady friend here."

Agnes hurried toward the booth and gave Alby a big kiss on the lips. I tried not to recoil. Mackenzie and I walked back to the counter.

"I can't believe him," I said. "What are those books telling him?"

Mackenzie hopped onto a stool. "That's ridiculous that he thinks Gus did it."

"Alby couldn't find those animals if they were sitting on top of his head," I said. Not that I should talk; we weren't having much luck either.

We ordered milk shakes and sandwiches, and Sam

joined us a half hour later. She looked exhausted. Her hair was messed up and she had a smear of dust on the side of her face. "I've spent the last six hours buried in Gus's files," she said. "I even poked through the ones in his locked cabinet. I didn't find much on Jack but I found something—an address for Victoria, his ex-wife. I think it's current. It's on the island of Capri."

"Wayne said Jack might've gone to Italy," I told her. "But I don't know if he was telling the truth or trying to lead us in the wrong direction." We filled her in on our conversations with Wayne and Frum.

"If Wayne does know where Jack is, how are we going to get him to cough it up?" Sam asked.

"We can torture him by tying him to a chair and making him listen to Top-forty pop music till he cracks," I said. Then I thought of something for real. "Did you see those postcards on the cash register? I wonder if any of those could be from Jack?" I shrugged.

"Maybe. But a postcard wouldn't have a return address. You could get a zip code off the postmark, though," Sam said. "That might be a start."

"But they're taped to the register and he's always at the counter with his book and LPs," Mackenzie said. "How could you get a look at the back?"

"I don't know," Sam said. "We need a plan."

Sam picked me up after school on Friday to pay our next visit to the Stinky Rose Pet Shoppe. Wayne was blasting the Sex Pistols so loud, we could hear it in the parking lot. We found him sitting behind the register dusting off a stack of old 45s. "Now, what can I do for you ladies?" he asked.

"You know we adopted a stray—she's who I bought the carrier and catnip for?" I said.

He nodded.

"She's having a hairball problem," Sam said. "At least we think it's hairballs. She barfs a lot, and just keeps coughing. It's terrible."

He scratched his ear. "Sounds like a hairball to me. Did you see any regurgitated hair in the vomit? Or blades of half-digested grass?"

Sam made a face—she was not overjoyed by this conversation. "Um—I don't know—I didn't look that closely," she said. "But we haven't let her outside lately, with everything that's been going on, so she couldn't have eaten any grass. It's probably hairballs. Do you have any medication that will help?"

I'd noticed the day before that the medication section of the shop was way in the back, far out of sight of the register.

"Sure. I've got a few things." He stepped out from behind the register and Sam followed him to the back of the store. She kept asking him questions about all the different types of hairball medication—he recommended the homeopathic concoctions most of all, and while he marched on past the rows of pet supplies and out of sight, I leaned across the counter and began to peek at the postcards as quickly as I could. They were stuck to the register; I'd brought a roll of tape to stick them back on when I was done.

A picture of the famous Hollywood sign was from someone named Liz who dotted her *i*'s with hearts. Sedona said, *Love, Auntie Hildy.* San Francisco was completely illegible and the name had blurred off the bottom. I unstuck the Las Vegas one from the register. It was of the Venetian Hotel. *The show's going well here— five more weeks in blue. It's no Hoosier Venice, but what can you do?—JJ.* I held my breath. I stared at the postmark. October 26, less than three weeks ago. The zip code was 89109. I grabbed a pen off the counter and wrote the date and zip and scribbled what the postcard said on my palm.

A couple minutes later Sam said loudly, "That sounds perfect!"—which was our code that she was finishing up the conversation with Wayne. I slapped on a piece of tape and stuck the postcard back up as quickly as I could. I shoved my hand in my pocket.

Sam and Wayne came back toward the front. I pretended to be absorbed in reading the packaging of a "How to Grow Cat Grass" kit by the register. Sam spent almost six dollars on Kitty Herbals Natural Hairball Formula, and she and I walked out to our car.

"Did you find anything?" she asked me as soon as we'd shut the car door behind us.

I smiled and read the scribble off my palm to her. "It's postmarked so recently—he must be there right now!"

"'Five more weeks in blue'?" she asked. "What's that mean? Are you sure that's what it said?"

I nodded. "I'm sure. Maybe . . . he's in the Blue Man Group?" That was a show that had been on Lafayette

Street in New York for years. My heart thumped. "Or it could be a theater term or something, like being in the black or in the red . . . I don't know. He has to be at the Venetian, though. I'm sure of it."

She nodded, and stared across the dashboard out the window.

"You know what this means," I said with a smile. "Vegas, here we come."

Eight

"If it was postmarked three weeks ago, he might not be there anymore, though," Sam said as we drove home. "The show could've been canceled, or moved on. And how do we know for certain that 'JJ' is him?"

"It's obviously him—that's what Wayne said he called him, and how many performers from Hoosier Venice can there be?"

She didn't argue with that.

"It's a risk, though," she said. "We could get out there and not find anything."

"You don't think it's worth it? Has Gus improved at all lately?"

She shook her head. "He came in to work today for half an hour. He had a bandage on his nose—he said he walked into a glass door at Video Paradise last night. He said they're giving him a year of free rentals not to sue, which makes him happy—he said he should walk into that door every year. But he took painkillers on an empty stomach, threw up in the bathroom, and went home."

"Sounds like he's doing fabulously."

"I know. You're right. We're going to Vegas."

At home, we checked the Venetian Hotel's Web site,

but the descriptions of the shows didn't list the names of any performers, and we didn't find anything blue-related. We looked up the Blue Man Group, and found that they were performing at the Luxor Hotel, just down the street from the Venetian. Sam perked up. "This could be it," she said. She clicked on several Web sites but none listed the Blue Man Group cast members in Vegas. She did find a Blue Man Group casting-call notice—the Vegas show was looking for performers between five-ten and six-one, with "athletic builds, excellent acting skills, excellent emotional range, charisma, passion, and eye sparkle."

"Sounds like him," I said. "He definitely has eye sparkle."

She smiled and shook her head.

The Luxor featured a massive black pyramid and gilt fake Sphinx. The Venetian had its own canal, glittery lights, and fake frescoes. Sam clicked on the rates for both.

She flinched. "Guess we're not staying there." The cheapest rooms they had were for $290 per night.

We tooled around online and found several travel packages that were much cheaper. "We should leave soon," I said, but then remembered that I had two big exams on Friday, in English and math. I wondered how Nancy Drew fit detecting into her busy school schedule.

We talked it over and decided we'd leave Friday afternoon, after my exams were over, and Sam booked a budget weekend package for two at a hotel called the Lovelorn Inn.

"That name doesn't bode so well," I said.

"But it's cheap." She paused. "What will we tell Gus?"

"That we're going to Cleveland to visit friends," I said. She sighed. "I hope he buys it."

"He's too out of it to notice anything," I said.

My head was filled with what we'd wear and do in Vegas—I pictured Sam and myself dressed in sequins and feather boas, playing roulette—and it was hard to put those thoughts aside and study short stories, literary criticism, and parabolas.

Thankfully Saturday night was a much-needed break: Leo's klezmer band performance. Sam, Colin, and I met Josh at the Clear Creek Coffee House on the campus of Wilshire College. The café had rearranged the tables and chairs so they encircled the platform where the band would play; there was a small space set aside for dancing in front. A sign behind the platform read:

CLEAR CREEK COFFEE HOUSE
WELCOMES
FIDDLER ON THE STOOP

Leo and several others were setting up their instruments, and Leo came over to us as soon as we walked in. He gave Sam and me big hugs. "I'm so glad you could come."

"We wouldn't miss it," I said.

"How's school?" Leo asked me.

"Pretty good—you remember my friend Colin?"

"Of course." Leo shook his hand. "Are you taking good care of Sophie?" Leo grinned—he obviously thought Colin and I were a couple, too.

Colin looked embarrassed, but didn't correct him. "Best I can," he said, and smiled.

One of the band members called Leo over, and he excused himself. Josh had saved a table for us right next to the band. Josh kissed Sam on the lips very briefly, and gave me a peck on the cheek.

"I've never heard klezmer before," Colin told Josh.

"Me neither." I shrugged like an ignoramus.

"I hope you like it," Josh said.

The music was fabulous. Leo played clarinet, and the band was made up of another man Leo's age on the fiddle, a middle-aged woman on the bass, and three young college students on the trumpet, drums, and accordion. I thought of the Museum Mile festival in New York in June, when Sam and I had heard Metropolitan Klezmer play outside the Jewish Museum.

I glanced at Josh. He seemed preoccupied; he stared off in the distance blankly, not even watching the band, with a serious look on his face. Sam noticed it, too. "Is everything okay?" she asked him.

"Yeah—I've got exams in a few weeks—I'm just a little stressed, that's all. Do you want to get some fresh air?" he asked her. Leo hadn't even finished his second song.

"Sure." Sam put on her jacket and followed him outside.

I relaxed in my chair, listened to the music, and

thought about Vegas. A smile curled at my lips. It was a big city—maybe they'd have good restaurants. (Knishes? Was that hoping for too much?) I was looking forward to that city-inspired, freewheeling, anonymous feeling that I'd felt in New York.

"What are you smiling about?" Colin asked.

"I'm just thinking about Vegas." I'd told him about the trip soon after we'd made the reservation, but he hadn't sounded particularly excited by the prospect of us going. He hadn't said why. He didn't look very happy about it now, either.

"You don't think we should go?" I asked.

He shrugged. "Do you think it's really such a good idea? I mean it's one thing when I'm nearby, or Gus is, but this time you'll be alone in a strange city."

It was nice of Colin to worry, but I had to resist the urge to roll my eyes. If he only knew. "We'll be fine," I said.

He looked wary. "You've been in hairy situations before, but you've always had some help around. And Vegas is a huge, depraved place. I mean, I know you lived in Cleveland, but Cleveland's not *that* big a city."

"I know. Cleveland's not that big." *Actually, I'm from a city of eight million people, you nut.* "But we can take care of ourselves. Really. We can check in with you and let you know how it's going if you're worried. When Leo said 'take good care of her' I don't think he really meant it that literally."

"I know." He nodded but didn't seem convinced. We sat back and listened to the band play.

"I like this music," I said.

Colin nodded. "Me, too."

It was amazing that we could have klezmer here, amid the cornfields. Several Wilshire students started dancing in a circle, in a sort of horah; a hippie college girl took off her Birkenstocks and began an interpretive dance in the center, her anklet bells jingling.

"That's a weird horah," I blurted, though my inner Queens girl slipped through and it came out *hawrah*. Not to mention the fact that I wasn't supposed to know what a horah was in the first place.

Colin didn't say anything; he just laughed and watched the barefoot girl shimmy to her own beat, her tie-dyed shirt a swirl of rainbow colors.

A few moments later my sister and Josh came back from their walk. Her face was flushed and she looked annoyed. When they sat down, they didn't look at each other. Was it a bad kiss? Too much tongue? I was going to nudge her to discuss it with me in the bathroom, but the band finished its set and Leo joined us at our table.

"You were fantastic," I told him.

Leo smiled. "Our accordionist lost his contacts, so he couldn't read the music so well tonight. But I'm glad you liked it."

"You couldn't tell," Josh assured him, and Leo patted him on the shoulder.

I felt a tug in my chest. I was happy to see him again, but I still couldn't help but wish that he had turned out to be *our* Leo Shattenberg. As nice as Wilda's Turkeyluck sounded, I'd still have preferred a dinner with family.

Although, of course, in that case Josh wouldn't have just returned from kissing my sister.

Leo drank a glass of water and a few minutes later the band reconvened for their second set. We all seemed to be daydreaming in our own worlds as they played; no one at our table said anything till the music ended. After several rounds of applause, Leo came back to sit with us, we congratulated him on the performance, chatted a little while, and then Sam, Colin, and I got ready to go.

Josh kissed Sam briefly good-bye. I wasn't sure if I was imagining it, but they both seemed stiff and stand-offish. As it turned out, I wasn't: as soon as we got home, Sam said, "Josh was acting really weird tonight."

"How?"

Zayde interrupted us with a loud meow; I leaned over and scratched her on the head.

"He started grilling me with all these questions. I mean he's asked questions before, but tonight he seemed almost suspicious. When did I graduate high school, when were our parents born, and when did they die . . . what street did we live on in Cleveland."

I took off my jacket. "Why was he asking all that?"

"I don't know." She sank down into the sofa. Zayde hopped onto her lap; Sam petted her absentmindedly. Zayde had somehow wormed her way into even Sam's heart.

"You don't think he suspects anything?" I asked.

"That's what I'm afraid of. This is *exactly* why I thought I shouldn't get involved with him in the first place."

"I'm sure he hasn't learned the truth." How could he have found out? Sam was always a little more on edge than I was, and I thought she was probably reading more into it than she needed to. Zayde let out a yowl, as if she was worried, too. Then I realized I hadn't given her dinner. I fed her some Tender Vittles, and Sam brooded in the living room, staring out the window.

Sunday evening was the Bring Our Pets Home vigil at the town square. A small crowd gathered by the gazebo, holding candles. Sam and I found Mackenzie, and we stood in the crowd together, watching. Wilda had set up a lectern, and she and Fern gave impassioned speeches in favor of the end of this rampant pet thievery, and encouraged people to pray for the quick return of the abducted pets. The biggest surprise was when Wilda said, "We would like to introduce a speaker who we added to the roster just today, after his sudden, recent tragedy."

It was Troy Howard, my first crush (and subsequently disastrous date) in Venice. Troy—football player, lifeguard, muscles-of-steel, brain-of-a-flea Troy—started blubbering at the podium.

"Fonzie!" he wailed. I'd met Fonzie, and despite his owner's less appealing qualities, he was a nice beagle.

Troy was much too upset to speak. He bent over the podium, his hand on his forehead. He paused and got himself together a little, then said, "Someone took my dog. Why? I ask you. Why?" He sniffed. "Fonzie is the best dog in the world. He isn't just a dog. He is my . . . my amigo. My friend."

I spotted Colin and Fred through the crowd, and we joined them. "Did Wilda ask you to speak, too?" Fred asked Mackenzie.

"I wasn't really up for it," Mackenzie said.

"Me neither," Fred said. "I'm not really sure what good this is going to do. Everyone already knows about the pets." He dug his hands into his pockets, looking depressed.

"When Fonzie was a puppy I tried to teach him not to chase his tail—'It's attached, Fonz,' I said. He wouldn't listen. He was always his own dog—" Troy's voice echoed.

"It's not looking good," Mackenzie said. "Yoda's been gone ten days now and no one's any closer to finding her, despite what Alby says."

Fred nodded. "Each day they're missing, it looks less likely that we'll find them."

"I wouldn't give up hope yet," Colin said. "Maybe when Sam and Sophie get back they'll find some leads."

Troy started sobbing, and Wilda escorted him off the stage.

"We'll try," I said. I felt bad that we'd made no progress in the pet case, and the situation only seemed to be getting worse. I didn't know what to say to Mackenzie and Fred. I gazed around the crowd, and my eyes settled on a man in a dark overcoat. I poked Sam. "Is that Gus?"

She squinted. "I think it is." We told Mackenzie, Fred, and Colin that we'd be back in a minute, and walked over to him. He was leaning on a parking meter. He'd grown a light beard and his eyes were bloodshot.

"What are you doing here? Are you feeling better?" Sam asked hesitantly—he obviously wasn't.

He coughed. "I was going for a walk and wanted to see what all the ruckus was about."

Alby took the podium. *"I will find your cats, your dogs, your bunnies, your turtles, your ferrets and I will bring them home!"* The crowd cheered a rallying cry.

"How's the case going?" Gus asked us.

I shook my head. "Not so good. We haven't gotten anywhere."

Gus shrugged. "They'll turn up."

I wanted to ask him how he knew that, or to tell him that they'd have a better chance of turning up if he'd help us look for them. But instead we just stood staring at one another, not sure of what to say. I smelled alcohol on his breath.

"I should be getting home. I'll see you at work tomorrow," Gus told Sam. "And then you're off to Cleveland?"

"That's right," Sam said. We said good-bye.

Gus didn't come in to work the next day, or the day after that. As Friday and our trip to Vegas approached, we became more and more convinced that we were doing the right thing.

On Wednesday evening I was studying for my exams, my books sprawled all over the kitchen table, when there was a knock on the door. Sam got up from the computer, where she'd been continually searching for signs of Jack Jenkins on the Internet—this time on every

Las Vegas entertainment Web site she could find.

It was Josh. His ears were red and he had a grim expression on his face.

"What's wrong?" I asked as he stood in the doorway.

Sam said, "Did something happen? Is it Leo?"

His eyebrows raised. "No—Leo's fine."

"What is it, then?" I asked.

"I just—I wanted to talk to you, before you went away."

"Come on in," Sam said, looking worried.

He took off his jacket and Sam hung it up for him. He sat down on the couch, his hands on his knees. He glanced around the room nervously.

"I'll leave you two alone," I said, hoping he wasn't about to break up with my sister.

I turned to go up the stairs but Josh said, "Actually, I'd like to talk to both of you."

"Okay." I turned back around and sat down in a rocking chair. What was this about? My stomach felt like a hummingbird was flying around in it.

Josh spoke slowly and evenly. "I've been thinking about this all week, and it's been driving me crazy, so I decided to just come talk to you and get it out in the open." It sounded like he'd rehearsed what he was saying. I sat on the edge of my chair, fiddling with my hands.

"A week ago, a man came to see Leo," Josh continued. "He was a private detective. His name was Hal Hertznick."

I felt as if I was about to fall off my chair and down into the earth.

"The *Jewish Daily Forward* ran a small story about

Ruth Brauner's painting being returned to her. Leo's name was mentioned briefly, and Hertznick read it and tracked him down. Hertznick said he was looking for two Jewish sisters from New York who'd stolen some money from their stepmother and run away. They had the same last name as us—that's why the detective thought Leo might know where the girls were. He thought Leo and I might be distant relations."

Sam and I stared at him, our skin as pale as snow, trying hard to remove all signs of panic from our faces.

"The sisters' first names were Samantha and Sophia, aged seventeen and fifteen."

For a full minute, the room was filled with silence. Sam folded her arms. Her voice was admirably level and cool. "And why are you telling us this?"

"Leo told the detective he had no distant relatives of those names, and had never heard of the girls before," Josh said quickly.

He'd stood up for us? I looked toward Sam. Surely we had to tell him the truth now.

Josh's gaze moved from me to Sam, waiting for our reactions. But we didn't say anything; Sam kept her expression blank.

"Leo didn't want me to mention it to you. But I wanted to. I wanted to make sure you knew that we both care about the two of you, and would never do anything to get you in trouble. He only told me about the detective because he thought I should know what's going on."

"And what do you think is going on?" Sam asked sharply.

"I—I don't know." Josh looked helpless.

Sam crossed her legs, then uncrossed them. "I can't believe you'd come here and accuse us of lying to you." She got up from her chair and stood across the room. "Whoever those two girls are, they're not us. I don't know how you could even think that we'd make up some story."

I couldn't believe she was saying this, still sticking to our story after it was so obvious that Josh and Leo knew the truth.

Josh's mouth opened, but nothing came out; he clearly hadn't been expecting this reaction.

"We need to get back to work," Sam told him. "Sophie has two exams and I'm doing research for our latest case."

"Okay." He seemed flustered, unsure of what to do. He got up slowly, gathered his coat, and walked to the door. He turned to Sam. "I guess I'll just . . . I'll call you when you get back."

She nodded silently, and shut the door behind him. Through the window, we watched him walk down the porch steps and into his car.

"What are we going to do?" my voice squeaked as he drove off. My heart felt like it was going to drop onto the carpet.

"I don't know. I'm going to call Difriggio." Tony Difriggio was our contact in the Midwestern criminal underworld; he'd helped us forge our new identities. She left a message on his cell phone, and he called us back just a few minutes later. I got on the extension upstairs.

Sam updated him on everything that Josh had said.

He thought about it for a while. "As far as I see it, you've got two options: relocate and start all over again, or get even closer to the Shattenbergs."

"Closer?" Sam asked.

"You need to be a hundred percent sure that they won't tell anyone who you are," Difriggio said. He paused. "No matter what, both options carry some risk. It's dangerous for you to be around people who know the truth, but it's also dangerous to run now. Running again could set off reactions—it would look suspicious to the town, to your friends there, your classmates and teachers—if you ran now they might put out more missing persons reports on you, which could get back to Hertznick and put him on your trail. You don't need even more people looking for you right now, in addition to your stepmother and Hertznick. Sometimes, if people are willing to help you out, you gotta take the risk and accept their help."

"Josh said Leo loved us—and Josh is in love with Sam," I blurted. We hadn't told Difriggio of this development before, but now it seemed like necessary information.

"He's not—" Sam started.

"He *is*," I interrupted. I told Difriggio how they'd been dating.

"That's good," Difriggio said. "That's perfect." I was suddenly enormously grateful that Sam was dating the boy who we originally thought was our cousin. The alternative—running away again and starting over—was something I didn't want to think about. I didn't even want my mind to go there.

"How can we be completely sure we can trust them, though?" Sam asked.

"You can't," Difriggio said. "It's a risk. Almost anything you do now is a risk."

We absorbed this in silence for a few seconds, and then told him about Vegas. Difriggio was not overjoyed that we were poking into Gus's private life, though he understood why we were doing it. He also thought it was good timing for us to take a trip out of town. He said Hertznick had been difficult to keep track of, but he'd try to get his people on it, to make sure our paths didn't cross in the future.

We thanked him for his help. He wished us good luck. We hung up the phone and I plodded down the stairs.

Sam and I exchanged glances. A part of me was terrified that she was going to say she thought the first option was a better one—that we should pack up our things right away and hit the road.

My voice wavered. "I hope we don't have to start all over again. I don't know if I can do it."

She nodded. "I know. We might have to, though, someday."

Friday morning I came out of my math exam with a colossal headache—after the Josh conversation I'd hardly slept for two nights, and had a difficult time completing endless logarithms and parabolic equations, not to mention writing long essay questions comparing Zora Neale Hurston and Alice Walker's writings. I'd done the best I could, but I was unprepared for the disconcerted look on Colin's face when he tapped me on the shoulder in the hall.

"Soph," he said. "Did you get my message last night?"

"Yeah—sorry I didn't get to call you back. We were busy packing, and I was studying and everything."

"I looked for you at lunch yesterday, too, but even Mackenzie didn't know where you were."

"I was studying in the library." I'd wanted to be alone. My mind had been whirring with thoughts of leaving Venice, of losing our whole new lives, of losing everything. I was so worn out from not being able to tell Colin and Mackenzie what was going on. In English class that morning I'd given Mackenzie our house key so she could feed Zayde while we were gone. She'd asked, "Are you sure you're okay? You've seemed so out of it the last couple days." The only excuse I'd come up with was that I was getting my period.

"Do you want to go outside? We need to talk—there's something I want to ask you," Colin said. His face looked stern and serious.

My heart thumped like a drum. What did he want to ask? *We need to talk.* He knew. Colin *knew*. I'd made too many slips—the *hawrah,* and a couple weeks ago in his shop I'd delightedly picked a book off his shelf called *Loxfinger: A Thrilling Adventure of Hebrew Secret Agent Oy Oy Seven* by Sol Weinstein, published in 1965. Colin knew. He'd probably had suspicions all along but kept them to himself, until now.

I wasn't going to give him the chance to even ask. "I can't—Sam's picking me up in a minute," I said. "Sorry!" I bounded out the door. Colin looked stricken. I ran toward the parking lot, where Sam was waiting.

Nine

We bid good-bye to our elderly Buick in the Indianapolis airport parking lot. As our plane took off for Vegas, I gripped the sides of my seat, then rested my head on my arms.

"I think I'm going to throw up," I said. I was bleary-eyed and exhausted from not sleeping, and jumpy and on edge from this whole Colin, Josh, and Hertznick thing.

"Colin might have wanted to talk about something else," Sam said, but she didn't know for certain. She was busy coping with her worries by compulsively completing a book of *New York Times* crossword puzzles, in ink. I watched the patchwork farms coast by below and then I finally fell asleep.

Four hours later, I blinked at the bright lights and clanging slot machines of the Las Vegas airport. Surprisingly, I felt a little better being in a new place, where I could put the recent events out of my mind for a little while.

"I can't believe you can start gambling right in the airport," I told Sam as we hauled our luggage through the thronging Vegas crowds. "People can't even wait to get to a casino?"

The air outside was warm and inviting, much nicer

than it had been in Venice. We picked up our rental car. It was a relief to drive around in something that wasn't decomposing with rust. We set out for our hotel.

We'd never been to Vegas before; we had no idea what to expect. I'd been picturing lots of glamour and sophistication—women in evening dresses and movie stars and glittery lights—sort of like a cross between TriBeCa and Times Square. What I saw as we cruised down the Vegas streets in broad daylight had a freakish, aging-Disneyland sort of quality, with bright-colored buildings, billboards, a gazillion "99 cent prime rib" (the mad cow discount?) and "cash your paycheck" signs, and tour buses releasing hordes of old people ready to gamble. The city looked seedy and sort of fragile, as if it all might blow over with a strong wind, like a movie set.

The Lovelorn Inn turned out to be a seventies-style place with shag carpets and silver plaid wallpaper that was peeling off the walls. People were gambling away at the slot machines in the lobby beneath fluorescent lights. The lobby also featured an exhibit of "Original Exquisite Art by Las Vegas Resident Marty Bicks," which consisted of velvet portraits of major American presidents shown holding hands with Elvis and/or Princess Diana and/or Jesus. These were on sale for the bargain price of $675 each. "Velvet presidents aren't cheap," Sam said.

The elevator was paneled in speckled mirrors. In our room, I stared at the green velour furniture and peeked under the mattress.

"What are you doing?" Sam asked.

"Just making sure there's not a dead body under there," I said. "All's clear."

She put her suitcase in the corner and sat on the bed. "Should we head to the Venetian or the Luxor first?"

"Let's try the Venetian," I said. We picked up tourist maps in the lobby and began our search for Jack.

"Oh my God," I said, half in awe and half in horror as we headed down the strip, past the Stratosphere, Sahara, and Circus Circus casino, which had a scary-looking clown on its sign. We neared the Venetian. The massive gilt hotel sprawled upward and outward, flanked by what appeared to be replicas of buildings from Venice, Italy, complete with a bell tower and winged gargoyles.

The lobby glimmered with blinding gold and sparkly chandeliers. Sam and I gazed up at the fake frescoes of half-naked ladies and frolicking cherubs, then found the information desk. The woman behind it, whose name tag said DEBBI, wore so much makeup it looked like the fresco artists had gone to work on her, too.

"Um, we're looking for a guy who might be a performer in one of your shows—Jack Jenkins," I told her hopefully. "Or he could be known as Jacques or JJ or maybe something else. He might be wearing blue."

Debbi looked at us as if we were escapees from a mental institution.

Sam flashed her Jenkins Detective Agency card. "We work for Jenkins and Associates," she said in an impressively professional voice. "We'd really appreciate your help."

Debbi glanced at the card.

"We're trying to reunite a father with his son," Sam said.

This seemed to affect Debbi, finally; she typed on her computer keyboard, then shook her head. "Sorry. No Jack Jenkins is listed in our staff database."

I showed her a photocopy of Jack's picture from the yearbook. "Do you recognize him?"

She shook her head again. A line was building up behind us; a woman waiting sighed audibly. "Girls, I'm really sorry I can't help you. Good luck," Debbi said. She nodded at the next person on line.

"But is there someone we could talk to who—"

"I'm sorry," she said forcefully.

We stood at the desk for a second, hoping she'd change her mind, but she ignored us. We left the lobby and wandered out toward the canal, which flowed through the Grand Canal Shoppes. "What now?" Sam asked.

"A canal with water in it," I said. "Shocking." I glanced around at all the stores. "Oooh, Sephora."

"Focus, Sophie, focus. This is a business trip. We're trying to find Jack."

I nodded. I stared at an actor behind a velvet rope; he was covered in white makeup, impersonating a statue. Other performers in Renaissance garb roamed around, juggling and doing tricks. "Maybe we can talk to one of these street performers. Maybe they know Jack," I said. It was a long shot, but worth a try.

We watched a man in a harlequin outfit with a large

fake nose juggle five orange balls to the ooohs and aaahs of the passing shoppers wearing fanny packs. When he finished his act, I said, "Excuse me. Could I ask you a question?"

"Hello m'lady! What-a can-a I do for-a you?" he bellowed in a mangled Renaissance-meets-pasta-sauce-commercial accent.

I blinked. Hopefully this was not Jack's performance gig. "I, uh—we're trying to track down a long-lost friend, an actor, and we wondered if he might be working here at the Venetian. His name is Jack Jenkins, or JJ, though he might be using a different name now." I showed him the picture, explained who we were, and gave him our business card.

"He's handsome," the juggler said, dropping the accent, thankfully.

Tell me about it, I wanted to say.

He kept staring at the photo, then shook his head. "Sorry. I don't know him." He noticed the disappointed look on our faces, then added, "Maybe Leif can help—he's worked here forever and knows everyone." He led us over to one of the living statues.

"Hey, Leif," he said. The statue reluctantly got down from his perch and came over to us. I tried not to stare at his chest muscles.

"These ladies are looking for a friend of theirs, Jack Jenkins." He showed Leif the picture.

Leif stared at it for several long moments, then shook his head. "He doesn't work here."

My insides sank. "Are you sure?"

Leif nodded. "I would've noticed him. He must be at another hotel."

"I guess we'll try the Luxor," I told Sam.

"You can call my friend Gary Struffles at the Luxor. He should know if your friend's there."

I brightened, and thanked him as he wrote down Gary's number.

We went down the strip to the Luxor, with its black pyramid facade and massive Sphinx head. Its cavernous lobby housed palm trees and Egyptian sculptures. At the front desk, the receptionist dialed the extension number Leif had given us; she spoke to someone, then told us, "He's working the bar at the pool." She pointed us in that direction.

The Luxor pool turned out to be four pools, complete with Egyptianesque columns spewing arcs of water. It made the Rose Country Club pool back in Venice seem like a puddle in comparison.

We made our way to the poolside bar. Before we could even ask the bartender his name, he said, "What can I get for you girls?"

"Uh, two banana daiquiris," Sam ordered to my surprise. The Vegas devil-may-care attitude was clearly seeping into her. Who cared if our new lives in Indiana were falling apart? Who cared if our secret identities were blown? We were in Vegas! But then she added, "Virgin daiquiris, that is."

"Are you Gary Struffles?" she asked him.

"I am," he said. He made our drinks and put two umbrellas in them. "What can I do for you?"

"Leif at the Venetian told us to talk to you." Sam launched into our Jack Jenkins spiel.

"We thought he might be in the Blue Man Group, performing here." I showed him the picture.

He stared at it. "He's not in the Blue Man show. They're having casting calls now—I tried out for it last week—but I haven't seen this guy's face or heard of him anywhere. Sorry."

This was getting depressing. Gary went to take an order from a woman in turquoise-rimmed sunglasses, and we sipped our daiquiris.

"I thought it would be easier to find him," I said.

Sam sighed. "I hope we didn't come all the way here for nothing."

"We just have to think," I said. "What would Sherlock Holmes do?"

"That would make a nice bumper sticker," she said.

We finished our drinks and my stomach made an audible noise. "Before we do anything else, we need to get some dinner," I said. "I can't think like Sherlock Holmes on an empty stomach."

Sam glanced at her watch. It was five o'clock Las Vegas time, eight o'clock our time. "Where do you want to eat?"

"I want to find a real Jewish deli." I turned to Gary. "Do you know a good Jewish deli in town?" What a relief it was to ask that without having to worry what anyone might think. A vision of Hertznick flitted through my mind, but I pushed it away.

"Schmultz's," Gary said. "It's the best." He drew us a

map on a cocktail napkin. "Glad I could help you with something."

As we headed back down the strip, I gazed at the skyline of the New York, New York Hotel. They had built a replica of the Empire State Building, the Chrysler Building, the Statue of Liberty, and the Brooklyn Bridge, all smushed together with a roller coaster. I actually felt a little homesick, staring at it.

"Do you want to go check it out?" Sam asked me, noticing the expression on my face.

"Nah," I said. It was a far cry from the real thing.

Sam and I gorged ourselves at Schmultz's delicatessen. We ordered matzo ball soup, pastrami sandwiches, blueberry knishes, and an array of pickles. I was in heaven. As I sipped my egg cream, all the worries I'd had back in Venice seemed a million miles away.

"I think if we just keep doing what we're doing, going to all the major hotels and asking around for Jack, we'll be sure to get a lead somewhere," I said.

"There are a gazillion hotels in Vegas, though," Sam said. "It could take us weeks to get to all of them."

"We've only been to two on the strip so far. We'll go to the other big ones tonight, and tomorrow we can check some smaller ones."

She shrugged, and noisily slurped the last bit of her egg cream through a straw. For a second, I felt like we were back at Katz's Deli in Manhattan.

"There were a few Jack Jenkins addresses that came up through my database searches that I couldn't confirm over the phone," she said. "We can check as many hotels as we can tonight, and then try the addresses tomorrow in the daytime."

"Sounds like a plan," I said. We shared rugelach and chocolate babka for dessert. I seemed to have grown an extra stomach just to accommodate the Jewish deli food.

That night, we cruised from the Sahara to Caesars Palace to Excalibur to the Four Seasons and most places in between, going through the same rigmarole we had at the Venetian and Luxor, with no luck. The hotels and casinos began to blur together into a smear of glitter and cheesiness. At Treasure Island we watched the free outdoor pirate show, a battle between the HMS *Britannia* and the *Hispaniola* pirate ship. We watched the faux volcano erupt at the Mirage. At nine o'clock—midnight our time—we'd made zero progress and Sam could no longer keep her eyes open. We headed back to the Lovelorn Inn and to bed.

I stayed awake for a while, staring at the plaid wallpaper, trying not to let my mind wander to Hertznick, Josh, and Colin, and wondering whether our visit here would turn out to be a total failure. I pushed those thoughts out of my head, and instead thought of Jack. I pictured him dancing onstage in the Venice High video of *Grease,* his voice in perfect pitch. When I finally fell asleep, I dreamed elaborate dreams involving Jack rescuing me from a nefarious pirate ship, both of us in Renaissance garb. After he saved me from the pirates, and the sea in which I almost drowned, he took me to the pool and gave me mouth-to-mouth resuscitation. I looked up at Jack's face as he was about to kiss me. But it wasn't Jack's face anymore. It was Colin's.

We ate our breakfast at the Lovelorn Restaurant the next morning, and spent half the day hunting down every J. Jenkins all over Las Vegas. We found an eighty-year-old retiree in a senior citizens' development, a fifty-year-old professional golfer, and a six-year-old boy. Obviously, none of them was our Jack.

"What should we do?" I asked Sam.

"I don't know. Run through the city screaming Jack's name? Drown ourselves in the Venetian's canal since we flew across the country for nothing?"

I stared out our car window. I'd been out of it all morning, thinking about my dream. Did I want to kiss Colin? Is that what the dream was about?

"I guess if we don't find Jack, it just wasn't meant to be," Sam said in a downhearted voice.

We were cruising through the outskirts of town. A sign on the road announced: ELVIS FAIR TWO MILES AHEAD! GIFTS & COLLECTIBLES GALORE!

"Let's stop," I said. "I want to get something for Mackenzie and Colin." When Colin had gotten back from a trip to London in September, he'd given us a Sherlock Holmes cap, a book for Sam, and a red leather-bound journal for me.

"You think they want some Elvis schlock?"

"They'll think it's funny," I said. "We'll just see what they have."

She shrugged and turned into the parking lot. The

Elvis fair featured Elvis paraphernalia of all kinds: Elvis watches, jewelry, shower curtains, pipes, dishes, even Elvis-shaped pasta. A schedule had been posted announcing the afternoon's Elvis Pet Look-alike Competition. There were all sorts of human Elvis impersonators on hand, too, from ten years old to sixty. Most of the people manning the booths had dressed like Elvis, too. As we walked along the fairway, a booth at the end caught my eye.

MEET SCHMELVIS

ASK HIM ANYTHING

GET GOOD ADVICE

ONLY 1 DOLLAR PER QUESTION

"Good God," I said. "Schmelvis?"

"It can't be," Sam said.

We walked over to the booth. A handmade poster exclaimed:

DID YOU KNOW THAT ELVIS WAS A JEW? HIS GREAT-GREAT MATERNAL GRANDMOTHER, NANCY BURDINE TACKETT, WAS JEWISH. ACCORDING TO RELIGIOUS LAW, JEWISHNESS IS PASSED DOWN THROUGH THE MOTHER, MAKING ELVIS'S GREAT-GRANDMOTHER, GRAND-MOTHER, AND MOTHER JEWISH. THIS MEANS THAT ELVIS PRESLEY IS A JEW.

"Who knew?" Sam asked.

Behind a card table sat Schmelvis, in the traditional white glittery Elvis jumpsuit and an exceptionally large ruby-studded *chai,* the Hebrew symbol for life, around his neck.

"How can I help you girls?" Schmelvis asked in a thick Brooklyn accent.

"Um, we're just looking," Sam said.

"Actually, we'd like to ask you something," I said.

Sam gave me a funny look and jabbed me in the side. "What?"

"I'm going to ask Schmelvis about Jack."

She folded her arms. *"Why?"*

"Because we've tried everything else. I don't know." I shrugged. "Harry Potter had a prophecy. Maybe Schmelvis can give us one."

She rolled her eyes and gazed upward. "Why can't I have a normal sister?" She muttered her frequent refrain.

"I often ask myself the same thing," I said, which was my usual answer. I turned toward Schmelvis, who was smoking a fat hand-rolled cigarette.

I sat down in the metal folding chair across from Schmelvis, gave him my dollar and told him the Jack story.

"A perfectly good dollar," Sam grumbled under her breath.

"So what's your question, babe?" Schmelvis asked.

I took out my notepad, where I'd written what Jack's postcard had said, and read it to him: *The show's going well here—five more weeks in blue. It's no Hoosier Venice, but what can you do?*

"That rhymes," Schmelvis said. "Is it a song or something?"

"No—it was just written on a postcard." I stared at

the sequins on Schmelvis's jumpsuit. "We flew all the way out here from Indiana, we've tried everything, and we can't find him anywhere. What do you think it means?"

Schmelvis nodded knowingly. "I know what it is."

"What?" I asked. "What is it?"

"Your friend there is in the pornography industry. Blue movies, or live blue shows. Yep. I'd put money on it. He's a stripper." Schmelvis sat back in his chair, satisfied with his diagnosis.

"He is not," I said indignantly. How could Jack be a stripper? It just didn't fit with what I'd learned about him—that he was extremely talented and smart (what strippers could recite Shakespeare sonnets?) and had big dreams. Moncrief had said that Jack would go far. He couldn't be naked onstage in Vegas (not that I would mind seeing him like that). But if that was the case, there was no way we could reconcile him with Gus. If Gus hadn't approved of Jack's acting, singing, and dancing, surely stripping wouldn't endear him, either.

Sam shrugged, as if Schmelvis's opinion was a possibility. "Maybe we should look into it," she said.

"You think?" I asked.

"We don't have any other leads," she said.

"Well, good luck to you babes," Schmelvis told us, and greeted the elderly lady behind us who had a question about her arthritis.

"I wonder how we should go about checking out strip clubs," Sam said as we walked toward the exit of the Elvis fair.

"I don't know," I said. "Can you even go to a strip

club if you're under twenty-one?" I imagined getting
thrown out of a club by a security guard as they checked
my ID. I pictured the police leading me off in handcuffs,
like a scene from *Cops* or *NYPD Blue*. That's when it occurred to me. *In blue*. Of course. How could I be so dumb
as to not realize it before?

Ten

"Of course he's in some show dressed as a cop," I told Sam as we walked back to our car. "I don't know why I didn't think of it sooner."

"I don't know why *I* didn't think of it," she said. "Although I kind of like the idea of him being a stripper. It's sort of funny."

"Not to Gus," I said.

"True."

"We need to go to the visitors' center in town and find out every show that has a policeman in it," I said. We checked our maps and located the Visitor Information Center on Paradise Road.

The place was filled with guidebooks and brochures for every hotel, restaurant, casino, and performance in Vegas; we talked to a woman at the help desk named Angelina Pitts who had three-inch-long fingernails studded with crystals. We asked her if she could give us information on any shows featuring cops.

"Hmm, we don't have the shows indexed by theme," Angelina said. "We have a list of titles, though." She checked the list; her long nails tapped the computer keys. "Nothing with *cops* or *policemen* in the title is coming up. Do you have a fetish or something?" she asked, a little too intrigued.

"Uh, no," I said. "We're looking for a friend."

"We get fetishists in here all the time, that's why I'm asking. People looking for shows with lotsa bare feet, women dressed as animals, that sort of thing."

"Interesting," Sam said.

"Let's see, though. I know a couple of shows with cops in them off the top of my head—there's *The Full Monty* at Excalibur, they're in cop outfits in that, and then there's that guy in the Village People impersonator group at the Pixie Hotel."

"We already checked the Excalibur," I said. Could Jack be a Village People impersonator? Not exactly the career onstage that I'd imagined for him, but at least it wasn't stripping.

"You know, my boyfriend Rocky took me to a casino once that had a sort of police theme, too," she said. "It was at the Moonlight Lounge on Sunrise Drive."

"Thanks," Sam said. "We'll check it out." I glanced at the clock on the wall. It was 4 P.M. We had less than a day left in Vegas. I hoped that one of these leads turned out to be right.

We drove to the Pixie Hotel first. The Village People show didn't start until ten o'clock, but we talked to the manager, who gave us a cast list and showed us the promotional photos of the construction worker, cowboy, biker, soldier, Indian chief, and cop. The cop was short and in his early forties—not our Jack.

We drove to the Moonlight Lounge next. It was a run-down place made of dirty mauve-colored stucco with a blue neon sign. One of the *n*'s had broken on the sign, so that it read MOO LIGHT LOUNGE. I pictured a bunch of cows in sunglasses guzzling cocktails at the bar.

No one answered the door when we knocked, but on the side of the club a sign advertised their AWARD-WINNING MUSICAL REVUE, MEN IN BLUE. My heart quickened. Next to the sign was a glass case filled with photos of the cast of the show.

In the middle of the array of color photos, my heart stopped. I stared at the leather police boots, police cap, uniform, and thick belt with a silver buckle, and then the soulful eyes and tall, lithe, dancing body of Jack Jenkins.

The door was locked; we knocked again but nobody answered. A sign said SHOWTIME 10 P.M. CASINO OPENS AT 8 P.M. The building was embarrassingly shabby, compared to the casinos on the strip. No wonder Jack had sent Wayne a postcard from the Venetian instead.

"We'll have to come back at eight," I said. "Then we can go backstage and talk to him after the show."

Sam peered at the locked door. "We have to figure out what we're going to say. We haven't even worked out a plan yet."

"I've been kind of rehearsing it in my head," I said. "I think we should say that we're just here to let him know what the situation is. That his dad isn't doing so well, that he needs him. That Gus obviously loves him and misses him and needs to be back in touch with him, even though Gus isn't quite capable of saying all that himself yet."

"I think you should be the one to talk to him," Sam

said. "There's a little problem, though." She pointed to a sign higher up on the door. My shoulders sank as I read it.

21 AND OLDER ADMITTED ONLY. MUST HAVE PROPER ID.

"Oh *no*." I glared at Sam. "I should've gotten an older fake ID." I was suddenly annoyed. "You got to be twenty-one. Why couldn't I have? Or you could've gotten me two IDs, a fifteen-year-old one and a twenty-one-year-old one, for situations like this."

"I'm sorry, but how was I supposed to know we'd be in Vegas trying to sneak into bars?"

I sighed. "I know. Still."

"And if I get you a fake ID, how do I know you're not using it to sneak into bars in Venice?"

"There are about three bars in Venice, and they're all populated by old men like Gus," I said.

"Maybe if you dress up you'll get in. You sneaked into clubs a couple times in New York, didn't you?"

I nodded. Sam had never approved of the few times my friend Viv and I had managed to get ourselves into elite clubs in the city. Thank God I'd packed my extra-high platform sandals.

"I guess if you can't get in, I'll take you back to the hotel and then I'll come and talk to Jack myself."

I let out a muted yelp, a sound Zayde might make. I couldn't have come all the way here only to miss meeting Jack.

"I'll get in," I said.

* * *

When we got back to the hotel, I began my full-scale primping operation. I bathed, shaved, exfoliated, self-tanned, and applied foundation, powder, mascara, blush, eye shadow, and polished my nails and toenails. I put on a black strapless dress that I hadn't worn since my friend Julia Schecter's sweet sixteen many months ago. I also wore fake diamond earrings that I'd bought at Agnes Leary's Romancing the Stone shop (She'd sold them to me half price—I think she was in a good mood because of her new relationship with Alby.) During all this, Sam took a nap. She dressed in her favorite outfit—jeans and sneakers—in about three minutes. We left to meet Jack.

There were already two long lines of people waiting to get into Moonlight Lounge when we returned at eight. A man with a Fabio-style mane of brown hair guarded the door and the velvet rope. Apparently the Moonlight Lounge was a popular place. We waited on line for over twenty minutes. Fabio eyed the clothes of the aspiring clubgoers; he opened the velvet rope every couple minutes and nodded a few people in, usually young women in outfits that could only be described as getups—a woman in a zebra-print dress with matching boots; a girl in a red leather jumpsuit. He nodded some people toward the second line, which apparently was for those who didn't make the first cut, but might make the second.

Sam and I finally neared the head of the line. I stood in front of Sam, and thankfully Fabio opened the rope and let me in, without asking for ID—my shoulders relaxed in relief. The time I'd spent getting ready, with the dress, makeup, and my upswept hair had clearly paid off. (Not to mention the Wonderbra I'd bought while shopping with Mackenzie a few weeks ago.)

I stood by the door waiting for Sam to join me. Fabio was eyeing her jeans and sneakers. He let two women behind her in, but not my sister.

"Excuse me," Sam said. "I was here before those women."

"They're on the list," he said.

"They can't be on 'the list.' You didn't even ask their names," she snapped.

He ignored her.

She glared at him. "I need to get into this club. I'm on important business here."

He pretended she didn't exist, and kept the velvet rope closed. Then he let in two girls with very low-cut tops, their massive breasts overflowing.

Sam realized what was happening. "This is ridiculous. Just because I don't dress like a strumpet you won't let me in the club? It's . . . it's sexist! I'm reporting you to the ACLU!"

"Um, excuse me a sec," I said to Fabio. I walked over to Sam and whispered, "You're pissing him off. He's never going to let you in at this rate."

"Why should that gorilla be in control?" she asked a little too loudly.

"Maybe you should slip him some cash," I said.

"I'm not giving Apeman my money!" she said.

"Okay," I said quietly. "Well, should I just wait for you inside? What if he doesn't let you in?"

She pressed her lips together. "I'll keep waiting, but if

the Simian doesn't let me, in I guess I'll have to go try to find something ridiculous to wear and then I'll come back." She reached into her pockets and handed me some cash. "Don't spend it all. And only drink orange juice."

"Okay," I said.

She gave me the cell phone. "If I still can't get in for some reason, I'll call you and pick you up at midnight. Be careful."

We hugged, and I went inside the club.

It was dark, smoky, and filled with slot machines, blackjack tables, and dozens of other gambling tables I'd never seen before. The only gambling I'd ever done was playing dreidl for Chanukah gelt, and poker with Sam for M&Ms.

The club had a mix of all sorts of people—old and young, though the uniting theme seemed to be tackiness. On the velvet-lined walls, a tiger stalked across a field. Disco balls swirled about. The carpeting had pictures of dollar signs and gold coins.

I dodged clouds of smoke and settled at a blackjack table near the stage, beside a woman in a hot pink dress that showed more leathery, freckled cleavage than I wanted to see. Her teeth looked like toasted marshmallows. I suddenly felt a little nervous being at a casino and club all by myself. I should have bargained with Fabio to get Sam in, too. But what could I have done? Shouted "Let my people in!" like a dance-club Moses?

The waitress came by. The guy next to me ordered a Sea Breeze. When the waitress asked me what I wanted I muttered, "Orange juice."

"I'm on the wagon," I explained to my tablemates.

The dealer set the cards down. I said I was going to just watch first.

Sam had given me thirty dollars, and I had ten of my own. On the next hand, I put down ten.

I won fifteen. "I love blackjack," I said.

"You're a natural," the dealer told me.

"Thanks. Actually, I'm here to see the show."

"It's spectacular," said the woman with the abundant cleavage. She introduced herself—her name was Regina. "I come here every night to watch it." She asked where I was from.

"New York City, but I go to college in Indiana." I thought that mentioning New York City would make me sound sophisticated, and college would make me sound older.

"Indiana! How'd you get from New York City to Indiana?"

"I wanted a simpler life," I said.

"I can relate to that," Regina said. "Your folks still live in New York?"

"No. Um . . . my parents . . . actually they passed away," I said. It was always hard to deliver such information in a regular conversation.

"Oh. I'm so sorry." She held my hand a moment, and then gave me some of her chips.

This was the Orphan Effect, as Sam and I'd been calling it; as soon as people found out we had no parents, they liked to give us things—food and free car repairs and rent discounts.

I played a couple more hands and won both. The

waitress offered me another drink. I asked for a Long Island Iced Tea, I had heard someone else order one and figured how much alcohol could be in something called an iced tea? I said, "Heavy on the tea, and on the rocks, please. With a twist."

"Sweetie, you sound like a high roller already," Regina said.

At ten, the lights went down and the show began. It was like a cross between the circus and a musical I'd seen at Radio City Music Hall when I was six. It started out with male and female cops fighting male and female criminals in an elaborate dance, including backflips and the occasional kickboxing move. I kept scanning the dancers' faces looking for Jack's, but I didn't see him anywhere. I started to panic. Maybe it wasn't him in the photo we saw. Maybe he wasn't in the show.

Then a policeman ran down the middle aisle of the club and somersaulted onto the stage. *Jack!* He looked a little older than in the Venice High videos, and even more gorgeous. I couldn't believe he was here, in person, twenty feet from me, on the stage.

Jack shouted at the criminals: "Gotcha!" Then he belted out a song about crime fighting and cleaning up the streets. His voice was entrancing, and he danced expertly to the hoots and howls of the crowd. He was the star.

At one point during the show, he took off his sweaty police shirt and swung it toward the audience. Regina made a dive for it as if it was a bridal bouquet, and caught it proudly. "This is the seventh time I got it," she told me.

Jack was even more handsome in person than he had been in the pictures and video. I couldn't stop grinning as I watched him sing and dance amid the smoke from the smoke machine and the flashing purple lights. I couldn't believe I was actually in the same room with him.

After the show, the "cops" circulated in the crowd to sign autographs. They seemed to hover around certain tables. Regina caught me staring at Jack while I played another hand. "The stars hang out over at the hundred-minimum tables," she said. "You want to meet that guy?"

"You know him?"

"Come with me."

We went up to the table where he stood. He had a new police shirt on; the buttons sparkled with rhine-stones.

"Regina," Jack said, and kissed her on the cheek.

"This is Sophie," Regina said. "She's a big fan. I'll leave you two alone." She pinched me on my arm as she walked away.

Jack stared at me. My insides flipped.

"You were so great!" I gushed. "Really amazing! Better than anyone on *NYPD Blue* or *Cops* or any of those shows!" What was I saying? What bizarre spirit of a Midwestern cheerleader had inhabited my body?

"Thank you. Is this your first trip to Vegas?"

I nodded. "I'm here from Indiana."

"Indiana? Where?"

"You've probably never heard of it. It's a small town called Venice." That's what I had planned to say when I met him. I hoped it sounded natural.

He blinked. "You're kidding me. I lived there, too. I went to Venice High."

"No way. Really?"

He looked away. "Uh—the manager's waving at me. Got to go. It was nice to meet you." And he was gone.

My heart fell. My plan had been for him to be interested in the fact that I was from Venice; then we'd chat a little, and then some more, and eventually, when the moment was right, I could segue into the issue of Gus. I hadn't expected him to run off after five seconds. At least he was still in the room.

The waitress brought me another drink. I sipped it while I tried to decide what to do. Clearly "the stars" were only supposed to talk to the rich gamblers—he was back by the hundred-dollar-minimum tables now. I had to get over there.

I went back to my seat beside Regina, played another hand, and won. To hell with Sam's mutual funds! She should give our parents' money to me to manage.

"Another Long Island Iced Tea!" I said when the waitress came by again, in what I hoped was an authentic Vegas tone.

I won another hand. I was getting pretty good at this. I kept on playing, and after a while (and with a few more chips that Regina kindly gave me) I had enough to go to the hundred-minimum table, where Jack was cavorting with the wealthier patrons.

I sat right across from Jack and smiled at him. "I can't believe you're from Venice," I said. He came over and stood beside me. I felt something warm travel through my body and settle in my stomach.

"I haven't been back there for a long time," he said.

"I've only lived there since July. You should come visit," I said.

He laughed. "Maybe sometime."

I was making progress already. *Maybe sometime.* "Sometime soon. Venice is such a great town," I said. "The landscape is really pretty, and . . . there are some great shops. Wright Bicycles, Etc. The Petal Diner."

"Wilda." He smiled. "Does she still run it? She makes the best pie on earth."

"I know," I said. "Have you had her rose-petal dough-nuts?"

He nodded. "They're delicious." He looked almost wistful. "I do kind of miss it there. Is that bar Muther's still around?"

I nodded. "Yeah, it is." I was about to bring up Gus when a woman in a silver dress at the next table held up her hand of cards and cooed, "JJ, I need your advice on what to do."

Jack excused himself and went over to the woman, who was dripping with cubic zirconia. I glared at her. I won my next hand, and they brought me another Long Island Iced Tea, on the house. I turned back and stared at Jack, and caught him glancing at me a couple times, too. I looked at him throughout the next few hands; a few times our eyes met and he smiled. Finally, taking a lesson from the woman in the silver dress, I said, "JJ? Um, could you give me some advice?"

"Sure," he said, and stood next to me. He suggested something but I barely heard what he said; my head had begun to pound. The room swirled. The dealer gave me another card and then started taking all my chips—I'd lost the hand and all my money. I suddenly felt incredibly dizzy. I held on to the table.

"Are you okay?" he asked.

"I think so. I shouldn't have had that last drink."

"You don't look so good."

"I'm fine," I tried to say, though the words wouldn't come out. I tried to pretend that the room wasn't spinning and fading away. I was suddenly aware of someone holding my arm, and then heard Jack say, "I'll take care of her."

The next thing I knew he was leading me through the stage doors and down a flight of stairs, to his dressing room. The couch was piled with about three feet of clothes. I lay down on top of them. The whole place smelled like feet. I felt like a three-hundred-pound man was sitting on my head. Jack brought me a glass of water; I tried to drink it but my stomach lurched.

"Did you drive here by yourself?" he asked.

"No." I moaned.

"Do you have any money left for a taxi?"

"No. Um, excuse me for a sec." I ran to the bathroom and threw up.

"I think I should take you back to your hotel," Jack said through the bathroom door.

"I—I have to call my sister." After I rinsed my mouth and splashed water on my face, I got the cell phone out of my purse and dialed the number of the hotel, which she'd programmed in. They connected me to our room, but it rang and rang. Sam wasn't there.

"Oh God," I said.

"You okay in there?" Jack asked.

I opened the door. "I can't get through to my sister. She said she'd pick me up outside, though . . ."

"At what time?"

"Midnight."

He looked at his watch. "It's two-thirty."

"*No.*" I sat back down on the couch. "She's going to kill me. I'm dead." Sam was probably talking to the real police, trying to put out a missing persons report on me right now.

"I can take you back to your hotel," Jack said. "Where are you staying?"

"The Lovelorn Inn," I said.

He put on a jacket, led me up the stairs and out to the parking lot behind the club. He buckled me in, fastening the seat belt at my hip. Then he got in on the driver's side.

I knew I should be mentioning Gus, but I couldn't remember the speech that I'd practiced a dozen times, and I was consumed by trying not to throw up all over his car.

"Are you going to tell anyone in Venice that you saw me here?" he asked. "Like Wilda?"

"Why?" My voice cracked. Maybe *he* would bring up Gus. "You don't want them to know?"

"I guess *Men in Blue* isn't exactly what I imagined I'd be doing when I came out here."

"You were so good, though! I loved that part— 'Gotcha!' Gotchagotchagotcha," I repeated. What was coming out of my mouth?

He laughed.

"Um—" I started to say something else, but it came out garbled. I began to cough like Zayde. "Can we pull over for a minute?" I said in a scratchy voice.

"Sure." He stopped by the curb, I opened the door, and threw up again on the sidewalk. It was mortifying. A driver careening down the road shouted, *"Drunk! Loser!"*

I groaned and sank down into the passenger seat. Jack patted me on the shoulder. I closed my eyes, and the next thing I knew he was leading me out of the car and into the hotel.

The synapses in my Long Island Iced Tea–addled brain began to fire all at once, and I suddenly knew why Jack was taking me back to my hotel room: he wanted to make out with me. My pulse raced. This was perfect. If he *liked* me, then he'd easily agree to return to Venice. I couldn't believe that Jack *liked* me. I had to brush my teeth.

"Are you feeling better?" he asked me outside the room.

"Much."

I unlocked the door. Sam was nowhere in sight. I excused myself to the bathroom, brushed my teeth, and wiped the smeared mascara from under my eyes.

When I returned to the room, Jack was sitting on the edge of the bed. I walked over to him, put my hands on his shoulders, then melted into his arms and onto his lap. "Jack," I whispered huskily. "Thank you for bringing me back here."

"Sophie," he said.

I closed my eyes and parted my lips, waiting for him to kiss me. Instead, he gracefully lifted me off his lap and placed me beside him. "I'm sorry, I didn't mean to give you the wrong idea," he said.

"Huh?"

"I wanted to make sure you got back okay—I mean, I knew you were underage and a little drunk." He smiled. "But I'm not straight."

"What?" In the foggy world of my first drunken night, this didn't compute right away.

"I'm gay."

"Oh." We sat there in silence for a second. "But—" I wasn't sure what I was going to say, but it didn't matter anyway since I had no chance to say it. There was a click at the door, it opened, and Sam appeared. Her eyes were bright red and she looked as if she'd been crying. She yelped when she saw me, then hugged me and started to cry again.

"Sophie, I was so worried. I thought something had happened to you. I waited at the club for hours and when you didn't come out, I finally got the guy to let me in and you were gone . . . I thought . . . you didn't answer any of my calls!"

She held me close to her. I almost never saw Sam cry; I felt horrible that I'd made her so worried.

"I'm sorry," I said. "I got a little sick."

"You smell awful." She peered out from behind my shoulder at the guy sitting on the bed next to us. *"Jack?"* She paused. "You got him to agree to talk to Gus!" she said, her voice suddenly happy.

Jack flinched. "You know my dad?"

Sam gazed at me. "Oh. You didn't—?"

I shook my head.

"Did he send you here?" Jack gripped the edge of the mattress. His face reddened.

Sam took a deep breath. "I guess Sophie didn't explain it to you." She gave me a look. I shrugged and grinned goofily. "We came to find you because your dad's in trouble," she said. "He doesn't know we're here."

Jack looked confused.

She explained who we were and how we knew Gus. "He's not doing well," she continued. "He's drinking, smoking, he's depressed, and he's spent most of his money searching for you. He hasn't recovered since you left. And the way he's been looking lately . . . if he keeps going like this, he's not going to be around much longer. That's why we wanted to find you."

Jack folded his arms. "How well do you know my dad? You know how he'd react if he knew what I was doing with my life—the cop uniform? Onstage? *That* would kill him."

Sam said, "I don't know. I think he'd understand."

Jack shook his head. "No. He wouldn't. Please don't tell him this, okay?" he said. "Please."

"I really think . . . I mean, I think maybe Gus has changed. If you could see how unhappy he is . . ." Sam said.

Jack sighed. "I can't believe you came all the way out here to find me. I never even met you before." He glanced at the clock on the night table. It was three-thirty in the morning. "I'm sorry. I need to go."

"Don't go yet," Sam said. "I mean—can't we talk about this a little more? I know it's late, we're all exhausted—but why don't we meet tomorrow over lunch or something? How about that?"

He paused, took a deep breath, and then nodded. "All right," he said. We made plans to meet at a place called the Blue Hippo at one o'clock the next afternoon. We said goodnight.

After he left, Sam and I just stared at each other. "So what happened with you two?" she asked me suspiciously. "You were on the bed when I came in."

"Nothing. Absolutely nothing."

"Really?"

"Jack's gay," I said.

"You're kidding me."

"Nope. Not kidding."

She smiled. "I guess it makes sense . . ." She narrowed her eyes. "So how much did you drink?"

"I don't know. I lost count. But it was all Long Island Iced Teas. How much alcohol could be in an iced tea?" I yawned.

"Apparently a lot," she said.

I peeled off my smoke-drenched dress, put on a T-shirt, and got under the covers. Sam climbed in beside me.

"Sophie, don't ever do that to me again, okay? You can't keep me waiting like that. I was so worried."

"I'm sorry. I won't. I promise," I said. She kissed my forehead, and I hugged her. I yawned again, and finally managed to fall asleep, once the bed stopped spinning.

In the morning, which still felt like the middle of the night, there was a loud knock on the door. I put the pillow on top of my head to block out the noise.

"What's going on?" Sam grumbled. The knock grew louder. "Some idiot must have the wrong room. Go away!" she yelled.

It was quiet for a few seconds, and then a man's voice asked, "Sam?"

"What?" Sam whispered. I sat up.

She got out of bed and opened the door. I squinted at the man standing in the light of the hall.

It was Gus.

Eleven

"*What* are you doing here?" Sam asked him.

"What are *you* doing here?" he asked.

"How did you find us?" she said.

"I believed your Cleveland story. Until I found your flight itinerary on the computer."

She gave him a quizzical look.

"Yes, I actually do know how to use the computer," he said.

"You do?" I asked. I'd only seen him peck on a manual typewriter with two fingers.

He made a huffing sound. "So what on earth are you up to here? And don't tell me Isabel the poodle was last seen gambling at Caesars Palace."

Sam and I exchanged glances. What could we say?

She yawned and shook her head. "We're really tired, Gus. You woke us up. We were up late last night and we've barely slept. Can't we talk about this a little later? What are you doing up this early anyway?"

"It's ten Venice time," he said.

"How about we'll go back to sleep for a couple hours, and then have breakfast? Okay?" Sam asked.

He nodded grumpily. "I'll meet you at the restaurant downstairs at nine-thirty," he said.

"All right." Sam waved good-bye to him and shut the

door. "I can't believe he came all the way out here," she grumbled, and got back under the covers. She set the alarm for nine. "What are we going to tell him?"

I grunted. "We'll think about that later," I said, and fell back asleep.

The alarm rang at what felt like three seconds later. I groaned. Sam got up immediately and poked me. "Get up, Soph."

I put my hands over my ears. My head was pounding even more than it had the night before.

"Rise and shine!" Sam shouted. She opened the curtains and light flooded in.

"Nooo," I moaned. I put the pillow over my face.

"Wakey wakey." She started to tickle me, her favorite method of waking me up when I was about seven years old.

"Okay, okay. I'm getting up." I staggered to the bathroom, ran a washcloth under the cold water, got back in bed, and put it over my eyes.

"You can have one more minute in bed and then I'm pulling the covers off. So what are we going to tell Gus?"

"We'll tell him we came out here for the Elvis fest," I said. My voice sounded like I'd just smoked ten packs of cigarettes.

"No, really."

"Then we'll tell them the truth and have them meet," I said.

"It's too soon. That would be a recipe for disaster." She pulled the covers off the bed. I screamed.

"Sorry," she said. "But we've got to figure this out. I think we should lie to Gus—if he knew why we're here, it would mess up everything. We'll just send him on his way. But when we see Jack, we'll convince him to come back to Venice for a visit. What do you think? Do you think we can get Jack to do that?"

I staggered out of bed. "I think so. He seems like such a sweet guy. It was nice of him to bring me back here last night."

Sam smiled. "It was. Especially considering he didn't exactly have romance on the mind."

I threw a sock at her, and laughed.

She took a quick shower, and then I plodded to the bathroom and took one, too. It only made me feel worse; now my head was pounding *and* wet. When I got out of the shower, Sam was brushing her teeth. Her eyes widened. "Yerr kin temmim seen trows," she said, her mouth full of toothpaste.

"English, please."

She spit out the toothpaste. "I've got an idea: You can tell Gus you came for a singing tryout, for a new teenage pop-star show."

"What?"

"It's a perfect excuse. He knows you sing, he knows you love TV. Of course you'd want to get on television, singing."

"Not on some dumb show," I said skeptically.

"Work with me here. It's a good story."

"Then how do I explain looking like hell?"

"You went out partying with the other contestants, of course."

"All right." I brushed my teeth, which felt like they'd been wearing furry sweaters, got dressed, and then we took the elevator down to the Lovelorn Restaurant. I kept the cold washcloth with me, pressed against my forehead.

"Do you really still need that?" Sam tried to grab the washcloth from me.

"Stop! I need it!"

She shook her head. "You're never going near a Long Island Iced Tea again."

"Fine with me."

I pressed the washcloth over my eyes.

The elevator doors opened and we walked into the restaurant. Gus was already in a booth, looking over the menu. "I can't believe this," he said. "Pancakes for eight dollars? That's four times what Wilda charges."

"The prime rib is cheap," I said.

"Even coffee's a buck fifty a cup. Highway robbery."

"So when did you get here?" Sam asked him.

"Last night. I took an evening flight, got here at ten, and knocked on your door but there was no answer. I came back later, but you still weren't here. So I figured I'd try again this morning." I shivered. Thank God Gus hadn't run into Jack in our room last night.

Gus sipped his coffee and gazed at us. "Now tell me why you said you were going back to Cleveland when you were really coming to Sin City."

"Sophie was embarrassed to tell you," Sam said. She touched my elbow.

"I auditioned for a TV show," I said. "They're trying to put together a new teen girl band." I shrugged. "I thought it was worth a try."

"Why couldn't you tell me that?" he asked.

"I thought you'd think it was dumb."

"Well, yeah, it is dumb. You're much too smart for that. But you could've told me."

"We didn't want you to worry," Sam said, "since we were going so far away. And we were right—I can't believe you followed us all the way out here."

"Only because I thought you were up to something."

"It was just a silly audition," I said. "Although if I make it on the show, it's a big deal." I tried to sound excited.

The waitress poured Gus a second cup. "I'm just glad you girls are okay," he said. "Two young women alone in Las Vegas." He shook his head.

"We're fine," Sam said.

Gus raised his eyebrows and glanced at my washcloth on the table.

"Sophie was partying with the other singers a little too late last night, but that's it. Anyway, we're going home this afternoon."

"Good thing," he said.

At the thought of going home, my insides turned over. That meant we had to return to the whole mess that I'd put out of my mind—Hertznick on our trail, Josh and Leo knowing who we were, and Colin either knowing or suspecting.

Sam drowned her waffle in maple syrup. "You're looking better than you have in weeks," she told Gus.

"I guess worry does that to a guy."

"You're flying back soon?" she asked.

"Five o'clock. On American."

"That's our flight," she said.

"I know. I found your itinerary."

"Oh yeah." She stared into her coffee mug.

"So how are we going to spend our last afternoon here?" Gus asked.

"We made plans to see my friends from the audition," I said, thinking quickly. "To rehash the whole weekend. We really kind of bonded during it."

"You going, too?" Gus asked Sam.

"Yeah—I promised them I would. I'm sorry we can't spend the day with you."

"That's all right. I can check out the sights for a few hours. I haven't been here in almost thirty years."

We ate our breakfasts quietly. I pushed my pancakes around my plate; I was feeling too nauseous to eat. It was strange to be with Gus in this wacky, glittery town. Venice had seemed so far away, but having Gus here reminded me that we'd be back there in just a matter of hours.

We finished our meals, and Gus paid the bill for us. "See you at the airport, then," Sam said.

"See you," Gus told us. We watched him walk out the lobby and toward the parking lot.

"That was close," Sam said when he was out of sight.

"I hope he bought it."

"I think he did."

The Blue Hippo had turquoise leather booths and multicolored hippos painted across its walls. It was packed with people. We sat at a table in the corner; ten minutes later, Jack walked through the door. He looked even more handsome in the daylight. He sat down with us.

"Feeling better?" he asked me.

"More or less." I'd finally, regretfully, discarded my washcloth.

"That was a pretty crazy night," he said. "I still can't believe you came all the way here to find me."

"It was important to us," Sam said. We didn't tell him that Gus had followed us to Vegas; we thought it would freak him out to know his dad was so close. We wanted to make him feel comfortable with the idea of getting back in touch with Gus, and then maybe we could arrange a meeting. Sam and I'd decided to ask him to come to Wilda's Turkeyluck.

We ordered sandwiches—I'd finally stopped feeling nauseous, and was looking forward to a grilled cheese and french fries—and we gossiped about Venice.

"Do you know that teacher Gerard Moncrief?" Jack asked.

I nodded, and imitated Moncrief's Shakespearean voice. "'Methinks reason and love keep little company these days.'"

He smiled. "Good old Gerard. Did you know his real name is Lester Honeybum? No wonder he changed it. How about Wayne, who owns the pet shop? Do you know him? He was on the AV squad in high school, and took the videos of all the shows I was in. One year some woman in a winter coat blocked half the production."

So it was Wayne who'd zoomed in on Jack's abs. I wondered if he and Wayne had been more than friends. I didn't tell Jack that we'd watched the tapes, since I didn't want him to think we were stalkers—sometimes there was a fine line between detective work and stalking.

We told him about the missing pets case—"Only in Venice," he said—and finally, we got down to talking about Gus. We told Jack the rest of our official story, the things we didn't mention last night—that we were from Cleveland, and our parents had died in a car accident. "The thing is, I can't imagine having a parent who's still alive but who we don't even talk to," I told Jack. "It just doesn't make sense to me."

"I know," he said. He stared at the table.

"Maybe you can come for Turkeyluck," I said.

"Wilda still does Turkeyluck?"

We nodded.

"I don't know. When I left Venice, my dad and I'd just had this huge, horrible fight. We both said some pretty awful things." He shrugged. "He never even came to a single one of the shows I did at Venice High. I mean, I know it was just high school, but . . ." He put his napkin on the table. "I thought maybe I'd see my father again when I was a success, to show him that he was wrong. But look at the show I'm in. He'd just be more embarrassed of me."

"He wouldn't be embarrassed of you," I said.

"Oh yeah? I'm sure he already is. Does he ever talk about me? Ever?"

I cringed, remembering how Gus had never mentioned Jack to us. "If you could see how depressed he's been—Wilda says since you left—"

Jack interrupted me. "He has a right to be embarrassed. I mean *Men in Blue is* embarrassing. My dad wanted me to be a cop, and not the kind who dances in a Vegas revue."

"You're really talented," I said. "I thought you were great."

"After you had five drinks and could barely stand." He mustered a half smile.

"But don't you think coming home is worth a try?" Sam asked. "You don't even have to tell Gus what you're doing out here if you don't want to."

Jack stared off in the distance. "I'll think about coming for Turkeyluck. I don't have any plans for Thanksgiving. It would be great to see Wayne and Wilda and Moncrief, whatever happens with my father."

We exchanged phone numbers and e-mail addresses, and reminisced about Wilda some more; Jack was smiling, but as he looked up, his features fell and his body stiffened. I followed his gaze to the front of the diner. Gus stood there, watching us.

"Oh *God*," I said.

Jack looked at us helplessly.

"Did he follow us?" Sam asked.

"He must have," I said.

"What's he doing here?" Jack's voice wavered.

"He showed up at our hotel this morning—he found out we'd come to Vegas and trailed us here—but he didn't know why we came, and we never told him we'd found you," I said in a pleading voice.

Slowly, Gus walked over to our table.

"Jack," he said quietly.

"Dad." Jack's face was grim.

"You followed us," Sam said.

Gus nodded. "I wasn't sure about that audition story.

I waited in the car for a while and then decided to come in. I think Jack and I should talk alone for a minute," he said.

We left them at the table and moved to stools by the counter. Sam hugged her elbows. "What a disaster. How did he manage to tail us? Did you see him behind us when we were driving?"

I shook my head. We stared at their table. We couldn't hear what they were saying over the din of the crowd. For several minutes it looked like everything was okay, like they were reconciling. And then they started yelling. We caught snippets here and there. People in the diner turned to look.

"You had no business running—" Gus shouted.

"If you'd just tried to be a little more understanding!" Jack's face turned pink.

"We've been through this before," Gus bellowed.

The fight went on for a few more minutes, until Jack stormed by us and out the restaurant, without looking back.

We returned to the table sheepishly. Gus looked pretty shaken up. His eyes were half-closed, his forehead was wrinkled, and he stared vacantly into space. I didn't know what to say to him. We just sat there quietly. After a couple minutes Gus finally said, "We've got a plane to catch."

"I'm sorry. We didn't mean—"

He cut me off. "I don't want to talk about it."

"But—we meant to have you meet later—we planned—it almost—" Sam stammered, and Gus looked away.

"I've got a rental car due back now," he said, as if the whole scene had not just happened. "I'll see you at the airport."

He got up and left the diner in a daze. Sam paid the bill, and we stared out the window, and watched him get into his car and drive off.

Sam buried her face in her hands. "What a mess."

I didn't know what to say. She was right.

At the airport and during the flight home—Gus sat in the row across from ours—there was an incredibly odd silence between us. Sam and I tried to broach the subject a couple more times.

I said, "Gus, we didn't mean—"

He held up his hand.

"Why don't we just talk about it," Sam said.

"I'm not discussing it," Gus said curtly. He ordered three minibottles of scotch, which he drank straight.

I didn't know how to correct our mistake. Gus seemed to want to pretend that it never had happened. When the flight landed, we got our bags and walked to the long-term parking lot. Gus's Chevy was parked a few cars down from our Buick.

Sam said, "I'll see you in the office tomorrow, then?"

He nodded. He got inside his car and drove away.

Our car, of course, took a few tries to start. "Who knows if I'll still have a job tomorrow," Sam said when the engine finally turned over.

Twelve

I didn't think things could possibly get any worse, but when we came home that night, we searched all over the house for Zayde and couldn't find her.

"Our lives have become a country-music song," Sam said. "We're orphans, my relationship's the pits, I'm about to lose my job, and now our cat's missing."

"Zayde!" I called out. "Zayde?" I walked into every room, searching under beds and chairs with a flashlight. I checked laundry baskets, the closets, basement, and attic, but she was nowhere.

"She always comes running when we come home," I said. My voice was thin. This was the last straw in all the events of the past weeks; I couldn't take more misery. I called Mackenzie.

"How was your trip?" she asked.

"We just got back and Zayde's missing. We can't find her anywhere."

"That's impossible. She was there this morning when I fed her, and I didn't let her out. The pets have only been stolen when they're outdoors."

"Not this time," I said, my voice cracking.

"I'm coming over," Mackenzie said. "I'm leaving right now." I hung up the phone.

Sam rubbed her forehead. "What if someone broke into our house?" We exchanged looks, ran upstairs, and checked under the braided rug and floorboards beneath it in the upstairs hallway, where the few things we owned that could prove our true identities were hidden. We sat back in relief: they were still there, untouched. I was grateful that I'd had my journal with me in Vegas; I had to be careful in the future to make sure that no one ever found what I'd written in there.

We started checking the locks and windows to see if they'd been jimmied, and then the doorbell rang—it was Mackenzie.

She gave me a huge hug. I felt like I'd been gone for two weeks instead of just two days.

"Did you find Jack?" Mackenzie asked.

"We did." I told her how Gus had surprised us also, and the whole messy story.

"What a weekend," Mackenzie said. "And then you come home and Zayde's gone . . ."

And she didn't even know the half of it. I took a deep breath and tried to stay calm.

She stared down at the floor. "There's still no trace of Yoda."

"No leads have turned up?"

She shook her head just as Sam called our names from the laundry room. We ran in; she was standing by the window. "Look at this," she said.

There was a hole in the window screen. We'd left two windows in the house cracked open so Zayde would have some fresh air, but they were intact when we'd left.

"Maybe someone ripped the screen and snatched her," I said.

Sam examined the hole. "Or she could have escaped herself. I've seen her claw at the screen door a few times. Maybe she wasn't used to being inside for a long time."

"But there's a pet thief out there . . . we know there is. They probably wanted to make it look like she escaped on her own," I said.

"It's possible," Sam said.

She got out her forensics kit—her high school in New York, the Bronx High School of Science, had a million different science electives, including one called forensic science. Sam had learned how to dust for fingerprints, which she did now, but she didn't find anything. "Just yours and mine," she said.

"The thief could've worn gloves," Mackenzie suggested.

The phone rang; I hoped for a second that it was Colin so that I could tell him everything that had happened—and then I remembered our last conversation, and the dream, and I hoped it wasn't him. The last thing I needed was him grilling me the way Josh had grilled Sam. I'd surely break down; I couldn't handle it right now. And I had no idea what to make of the dream.

It didn't matter anyway; it was Wilda. "You're back! Guess what? I have the best news. Guess who's here in my lap? Betty!"

"What?" I breathed.

"Alby found her."

"You're kidding me. Alby found Betty," I told Sam and Mackenzie; they went upstairs to get on the extension.

"And Isabel, too. Oh my Lord—Betty's purring so loud the whole house is shaking."

"How did Alby find them?" I asked incredulously.

"Well. Believe it or not" —she lowered her voice as if this was a tapped line—"he's found evidence of a whole pet-stealing *ring*. Just like I told you I'd seen on the news a long time ago. Apparently our town isn't the only one that's been hit this summer—Pritchett had a pet disappear, too. It was written up in the newspaper. This band of pet thieves has been striking small towns all over the Midwest. Do you know, Alby's not a bad detective after all, despite the things I've said about him in the past."

"What about Yoda?" Mackenzie asked.

"No sign of her yet. But he's sure he'll get her back soon."

I told Wilda about Zayde.

"Don't worry," she said. "He'll find her."

"So who's running this ring?" Sam asked.

"Nobody's sure exactly. Alby almost caught them. He saw two guys in a car on the road with Isabel and Betty in the back—he said he recognized Isabel's curls and Betty's sleek black fur right off the bat. He followed them in a high-speed chase and finally they ended up on Mitchell's road, out by the Mitchell soybean farm? There was a big fight—Alby's been studying aikido in Indy, did you know that? The men escaped, but Alby was able to rescue the pets."

"I can't believe Alby did that." I tried to picture plump,

uncoordinated, bungling Alby fighting off these men and saving the poodle and cat. Of course letting the men get away did seem like something he would manage to do.

"He said rescuing Betty and Isabel and transporting them to safety was more important to him than arresting the thieves. I'm so glad he didn't put Betty's life at risk just to capture them."

"He really thinks he'll find the other pets?" I asked.

"Don't worry about Zayde. I'm sure he'll find her."

We said good-bye and hung up. Sam, Mackenzie, and I sat down in the kitchen.

"I don't know. I'm not as confident in Alby as Wilda is," Sam said. "It sounds like a coincidence that he ran into those guys."

"Can you picture Alby in a high-speed car chase, and using aikido moves on two thieves?" I asked.

Mackenzie shook her head. "But I don't care how he does it, so long as he gets Yoda and Zayde back."

On Monday I spent lunch period in the library. I wanted to avoid seeing Colin; I didn't want him to start asking me questions about who I was until I figured out how to handle it. I also wanted to send Jack an e-mail. I settled down at the library computer and wrote:

———Original Message———
From: sophscottvenice@hotmail.com
To: jjdancer@yahoo.com
Sent: Monday November 24, 2003 12:21 PM
Subject: apologies

Hi Jack,

I just wanted to let you know how bad I feel about the way things turned out. It was so great to meet you and we hadn't planned for it to go the way it did. We didn't tell you Gus had followed us to Vegas because we didn't want to freak you out, and we didn't want you to have to see him with no warning. I'm sorry it turned into a fight. I know it's our fault, and I wish there was something we could do to fix it.

I hope you won't totally give up on the idea of coming to Venice for Turkeyluck. We'd love to see you again, and so would Wilda and Wayne and Moncrief . . . and your dad, even though he has absolutely no idea how to say it. My dad used to always drill into us: "Family is the most important thing in the world." I know it's true, and I hope you'll at least consider coming back . . . if for no other reason than that Wilda's decided to make EIGHT different pies this year, and her famous rose-petal doughnuts!

Yours in Venice,
Sophie

A few minutes after I pressed the send button, some-one said, "Here you are."

It was Mackenzie. "I've been looking all over for you. Colin's looking for you, too. He wants to talk to you."

My heart dropped. "Really?" I didn't tell her that's why I was hiding out in the library.

"Do you know what he wants to talk to you about?"

"No," I lied. How was I going to deflect his accu-sations? My neck prickled. Had he confessed his suspicions to Mackenzie, too? I searched her face to see if she seemed to know something.

A smile curled at the corners of her mouth. "Don't look so nervous. You should be thrilled."

"What?"

She grinned. "He wants to tell you that he has a *huge* crush on you," she blurted.

"What?" I practically fell off my chair.

The librarian shushed us.

"Well, he probably wouldn't use those words exactly," she whispered. "He would kill me if he knew I was telling you this. But I thought you should be prepared so you can figure out how you feel—if you like him, or if you need to find a way to let him down easy."

I stared at the shelves of books. Colin *liked* me? That couldn't be right. I was so relieved at the possibility that he didn't suspect who we were, I couldn't really absorb what she was saying.

"I think he wanted to tell you how he felt because he just couldn't take being only friends anymore, watching you run off after Jack and Pete and Troy."

"I didn't run after Jack. Anyway, he's gay."

"I told Colin that." She noticed my bewildered expression. "Haven't you ever noticed the way Colin looks at you?" she asked.

"No."

She shook her head. "He stares at you as if the sun rises and sets behind your head."

I fiddled with the strap of my book bag. "I don't know what you're talking about."

"Trust me. I'm not making it up."

"What should I do?"

"Just tell him the truth. How do you feel about him?"

"I—I'm not sure." What was the truth? I actually felt more nervous now than I had when I thought he knew my secret. I wondered if I should I tell her about the dream I'd had about him. That must mean I liked him—didn't it? But if our friendship turned into something else, what would it mean? Would we still be friends—could we still play Boggle and Lorna Scrabble and solve cases together?

I wished there was a machine you could step into that would give you relationship experience. I didn't know how to do this. With Colin, it wouldn't be like the crushes I'd had on Troy, Pete, and Jack, who I didn't really know, and who didn't know me. But did Colin even really know me? If we got even closer, would he find out the truth?

"Well, I think you're crazy if you don't go for him. He's such a great guy. But if that's definitely not what you want, you should tell him that. It's not fair to string him along."

I nodded.

"And then he could be free to fall for someone else . . . he'd make someone a really great boyfriend." Her eyes glinted. I looked up at her. From the way she said it, it sounded like she had a crush on Colin.

There was an awkward pause between us. I didn't know what to say. The bell rang. "I—I'll see you later," I said, and headed to my next class, feeling so confused that I walked to the wrong side of the building.

* * *

At dinnertime, Alby was holding court in the Petal Diner, soaking up the accolades for finding Betty and Isabel. Agnes perched on a stool by the counter and gazed at her man admiringly.

"So the two perps got out of their car, and I got out of mine. I faced them off like this." Alby squared his legs. "They weren't armed, and I had my club." He motioned some quick aikido moves, which looked like a cross between waltzing and a *Star Wars* fight scene. He twisted his arm as if he was choking an imaginary man's head. "You see, I had one perp like this . . . and then BAM!" He motioned a kick to an imaginary person's groin. "I knocked the other one down. I ran to their car, grabbed Isabel and Betty, and got away before the perps got up. You should've seen it."

People nodded; a few patted him on the back. Wilda had hung up a sign over the counter that said WELCOME BACK, BETTY! decorated with the signatures of about thirty different people from town. Betty herself was curled up in a ball by the window, asleep, oblivious to the ruckus occurring on her behalf.

After the crowd dispersed, Alby sat next to Agnes and started munching on a package of jerky. Sam and I plopped into a booth.

"Did Gus come into the office today?"

She shook her head. "Nope. I left him a few messages but he didn't call me back."

Wilda came by to take our order. She had a "Welcome Back, Betty!" button pinned to her apron. "Did you file a report with Alby about Zayde yet?"

"No," I said.

"You need to do that. Alby!" She called him over. "You've got to find Sam and Sophie's cat."

Alby waddled over to our booth; the Atkins diet and aikido classes had yet to change his figure. I couldn't help but think of how much better Jack looked in a police uniform than Alby did.

"How can I help you ladies?" he asked. We told him all about Zayde. He looked befuddled—his usual expression—and then wrinkled his brow and set down his jerky. He took out his notepad and wrote down the identifying details of our cat.

"Gray tabby, skinny, green eyes, long neck, about eight pounds," he repeated as he wrote. "Coughs a lot. I'll do my best."

"Thanks," I said.

Sam squinted at Alby. "So what did the perps look like? Did you catch their license plate, or the make and model of their car?"

Alby shifted in his seat. "I'm sorry, girls, but that's top-secret police information. Classified."

I sighed. That's exactly what he'd said about the swatch of cloth Fern had found. "Did you ever get a match for the evidence in Fern's yard?"

"That information's also classified, until official charges are pressed." He nodded, and returned to Agnes.

Wilda came back to our table with steaming bowls of chicken noodle soup. "Did you tell him all the details?"

"We did," Sam said. She put her napkin on her lap.

"What was the name of that town where the other pet was stolen?" Sam asked her.

"Pritchett, about twenty miles from here," she said. "Someone took an elderly lady's cat. It was written up in their paper. Alby had a copy of it and showed it to me. He hasn't found that cat either yet, but he's confident he will."

We sipped our soup—it was delicious, although I had a pang of longing for the matzo balls we'd eaten in Las Vegas.

An hour later, we were about to leave the diner when we heard barking at the door. Fern came bustling in with Isabel. The poodle had a pink glittery collar on, and the puffs on her head, tail, and ankles were neatly trimmed.

"We just wanted to come by and thank you again," Fern said. Isabel barked at a couple men in a booth, but went up to Alby eagerly and licked his hands.

"Oh, look! She knows you're her hero," Fern said. "Isabel usually barks at all men. She's a bit of a radical feminist, I guess. Oh Izzy. Sweet Izzy." She hugged her dog and gave her a big kiss.

"Isabel and I bonded when I rescued her," Alby said proudly. "Jerky anyone?" He offered the package around to us. Everyone refused except Isabel, who attempted to eat the entire package.

Sam looked at Alby. "Hey, um, Wilda said a cat was stolen from Pritchett, too?"

"I suspect the thieves have left Venice and are headed on a Midwestern rampage," Alby said. "So if you'll excuse me now, I'm off to try and catch them, and to rescue the rest of the pets." Alby scratched his belly, and he and Agnes left the diner arm in arm.

We petted Isabel on the head, then said good-bye to Fern and Wilda.

"I'd like to know why a pet case is classified information," Sam said as we walked down the street.

"I think Alby just doesn't want to share the limelight." I wrapped my coat more closely around me; the weather was growing cold. "I can't believe we're actually entrusting that man with the search for our cat."

"He's had better luck than we have, whether or not his story about those fight moves was true."

"Alby was definitely embellishing it. I mean—how could that man fight off two guys at once?" I asked.

She shook her head. "I bet he found Isabel and Betty walking along the road or something. I think he's just lucky." She put her hat on. "Maybe this whole pet stealing thing was a teenage prank or something . . . maybe someone let the pets out of their yards as a joke, and Alby's been lucky enough to find them. He's just been in the right place at the right time."

"Not lucky enough to find Zayde, though." I sighed. I thought about telling her about my talk with Mackenzie in the library, then decided against it. I was too confused—I didn't need Sam's advice on top of everything else. Instead I said, "I sent Jack an e-mail today."

"You did? What did you say?"

I told her what I'd written in the message. "I guess I thought it was worth a try."

"I'm glad you did. You know I was on the computer at

work today and I checked the recent Internet searches. Last night Gus looked for information about Jack online."

"Maybe he's considering getting back in touch with him again," I said hopefully.

"I hope so. But I wouldn't count on it."

Thirteen

I logged onto the computer and checked my e-mail as soon as we got home. I was happy to see that Jack had written me back.

——Original Message——
From: jjdancer@yahoo.com
To: sophscottvenice@hotmail.com
Sent: Monday November 24, 2003 3:50 PM
Subject: re: apologies

Sophie,
Thanks for taking the time to write to me. I appreciate it. I also appreciate you and your sister coming all the way to Vegas to find me. Don't worry, I don't blame you for what happened with my father. I just don't know if he and I can see each other without fighting.

I'll think about Turkeyluck.
JJ

"He's thinking about it!" I told Sam. "He's thinking about coming to Turkeyluck."

She read his message over my shoulder. "I hope he means it. At least he doesn't blame us."

I wrote him back a quick message.

——Original Message——
From: sophscottvenice@hotmail.com
To: jjdancer@yahoo.com
Sent: Monday November 24, 2003 7:50 PM
Subject: turkeyluck

JJ,

Glad you're still considering Turkeyluck! We promise it will be the best meal you've ever eaten. And Betty's been found! Also, if you decide to come, and want to tell your dad, or if you just want to get in touch with him sometime, here's his e-mail: GJenkinsAgency@hotmail.com. No pressure, of course.

There's a big slice of pie and a rose-petal doughnut waiting, with your name on them.

xo soph

After I sent it, Sam took over the computer and searched the online edition of the *Pritchett Recorder* for the article about the pets. After several minutes, she found it.

BAND OF PET THIEVES STRIKE MIDWEST

Vera Castleberry's cat Fluffy was dear to her heart. "Fluffy is my best friend," Miss Castleberry, who is 89 years old, said on Friday. "I tell her everything. All my secrets, things I'd never tell another soul."

Unfortunately Fluffy was taken from Miss Castleberry's home on Pine Lane Friday morning. The thieves had replaced Fluffy with a stuffed cat doll on the porch. Miss Castleberry, who is legally blind, didn't notice that Fluffy had been replaced until late in the afternoon.

"I just thought she was sleeping," Miss Castleberry said.

I read the article over Sam's shoulder. "It's like that movie *Ace Ventura*," I said. "Didn't Jim Carrey replace a dog with a stuffed animal?"

"I never saw it," Sam said. "I don't know how you can watch those dumb movies."

I was about to defend the beauty of mindless comedies when the phone rang. It was Fred. "Hey! I'm at work, and I'm inviting everybody to come over. Guess what?"

"What?"

"Guess who's with me? Herman! Alby returned him half an hour ago."

"You're kidding me. Alby was just in the diner. How did he find Herman in the last hour?"

"Wait—I've got a customer. Do you want to come over? Mackenzie and Colin are on their way. We're having a little Herman reunion."

My heart lurched at the mention of Colin's name—we hadn't seen each other since I'd talked to Mackenzie, and I still wasn't sure what to do.

"Okay. We'll be there in a minute," I said. I hung up the phone. "Alby found Herman," I told Sam.

She wrinkled her nose. "How did he do that?"

"I don't know. Let's go see Fred and find out."

We drove to Video Paradise. Mackenzie and Colin were already there, standing by the rack of candy bars and microwave popcorn. I said hi and smiled at them; Mackenzie smiled back but Colin looked away and petted Herman. My throat dried up. Had Mackenzie told him what I'd said—that I didn't know how I felt? Did she just want him for herself? Had my life suddenly turned into an episode of a teen drama on the WB?

"How did Alby find him?" Sam asked Fred. "Did he catch who did it this time?"

Fred shook his head. "He found Herman on the highway—Herman must have gotten away from the thieves somehow. Alby said he's been cruising the streets looking for the culprits. I knew Herman would get away. What a good dog." He patted Herman on the rump, and Herman put his paws on Fred's lap.

"Did he say anything about Zayde?" I asked.

"Or Yoda?" Mackenzie asked.

"No," Fred said. "I'm sorry."

Colin put his hand on Mackenzie's shoulder. He whispered something to her and she giggled. My stomach turned over. Had Mackenzie read Colin's feelings wrong—did he like her all along, not me?

I thought of my dream of kissing Colin, and I felt a sob rise in my throat. I did like him. I did. Why did it take me so long to realize it, until it was too late?

I tried not to think about it. I looked away and stared at the racks of videos along the walls. *Police Academy 2, 3,* and *4* were facing outward from the comedy aisle. I thought about Jack in his police uniform. Then I remembered the blue swatch of material in Fern's yard, and a thought occurred to me.

"Has Alby checked out *Ace Ventura* anytime recently?" I asked Fred. I tried not to look at Colin and Mackenzie.

"Why does it matter?" Fred asked.

"I just—I'm just curious. Can you look it up?"

"Sure." He fiddled with the computer, pressing buttons, and then said, "He did. On November fifth. A two-night rental."

"That's the day Yoda disappeared," Mackenzie said.

"Do you know where Alby lives?" I asked.

"He's got a new place, you know, he moved out from his mother's. I have his new address on his membership form," Fred said. He checked on his computer and then wrote the address down for us.

"Thanks," I said. "We need to go check something out."

Sam gave me a questioning look and followed me out to our car. "What exactly are we checking out?"

"Do you remember that Sherlock Holmes story 'Silver Blaze'?" I asked as she fastened her seat belt. Our father used to read it to us; it was his favorite Sherlock Holmes story.

"Of course," Sam said. "The barking dog that doesn't bark."

"Exactly," I said. "And do you remember how Isabel—who hates all men, and barked like crazy at Sherman Frum and every other guy she's met—reacted when she saw Alby?"

Sam's eyes widened. "Oh my God. Of course—she knew him. She had to have spent a lot more time with him than a few minutes in a squad car."

We sped to Alby's house, which was in a rural part of town, surrounded by woods; the nearest house was a mile away. We parked off the road, out of sight, so he wouldn't see our car. There were no windows to his garage; we couldn't tell if his car was there or not. We went up to the front door and knocked. No answer. It was nine o'clock.

"Maybe he's asleep," I said.

"I doubt he'd have returned Herman less than an hour ago and gone right to bed. Maybe he's staying at Agnes's," Sam said.

The front door was locked. We went around to the back of the house, through a fenced-in yard. On the way we passed three garbage cans; Sam peeked inside and held her nose. "This is my least favorite part of detective work," she said.

The garbage cans overflowed with empty packages of meat. Bacon and hotdog packages, chicken wrappers, jerky bags, massive Styrofoam trays that had once held ground beef, and huge industrial-size cans of tuna and chicken.

"That's really disgusting," I said. "The guy's going to have a heart attack from all that meat."

We walked around to the back door but it was locked also. There was a doggy door carved into the bottom of it. I gave Sam a look.

She knelt down and opened the flap. "I think you could fit through there."

"No way."

"Just try."

I felt like the girl from "Hansel and Gretel" being

stuffed into the witch's oven. I just made it through, wiggling on my hands and knees. I unlocked the kitchen door. Sam was about to come in, but then changed her mind. "Just look for the pets—I'll stand guard out here," she said.

I prayed that Alby wasn't asleep inside, and wouldn't wake up to find me breaking and entering. I crouched along the floor of the kitchen, and peered around. I didn't see or hear any pets. I walked into the living room. It was sparsely furnished with burnt orange carpeting and wood paneled walls. I crept around the corner. The door to the bedroom was closed. My heart pounded. I took a deep breath and opened it quietly. The bed was empty, except for a small speckled ball of fur curled on the pillow.

Yoda.

I scooped her up in my arms, and then I heard a faint barking. It was coming from the basement. I walked down a flight of steep stairs, opened a door, and Fonzie came barreling toward me. The basement was covered in foam egg-carton soundproofing material. In the center of the room, sleeping in a cardboard box, was a fat, hairy white cat—the cat from Pritchett.

"Fluffy?"

She perked her ears and gazed at me. I lifted her with my free arm as she meowed. "Zayde?" I called. "Zayde?"

I searched the rest of the basement and walked back upstairs, the two cats in my arms and Fonzie at my heels, calling Zayde's name, but she was nowhere.

Sam looked through the window and saw me with

the animals. She opened the kitchen door; Fluffy yowled as Yoda batted her on the head with her paw.

"I'm calling Gus," Sam said.

Gus came over right away. He called Alby's brother Callowe, who was the chief of police, and the two met us at Alby's house just as Alby's own car pulled into the driveway. As Alby walked up the front steps, his brother was shaking his head.

"I just located them tonight," Alby said desperately. "I was going to return them . . ." His feeble voice trailed off.

Gus and Callowe talked to Alby in the bedroom for a while, with the door shut. We heard Alby's occasional weeping through the wall as Sam and I sat on the couch, Yoda in my lap and Fluffy in hers. Fonzie ran around the living room, his tail wagging wildly.

After a while, Gus came out and said he and Callowe had convinced Alby that his reputation wouldn't be completely ruined if everyone knew the truth. There would be some punishment, but hopefully it wouldn't be too severe.

"Why did he do it?" Sam asked Gus.

"It started when he saw Yoda walking down the highway a few weeks ago. Apparently she'd wandered far away from the Allens' farm. Alby picked her up so she wouldn't get hit by a car, and was about to return her when he got an idea. He decided if he became a pet detective he'd get the respect he's always wanted—he'd seen some ridiculous movie or something that put this idea in his head." Gus rolled his eyes. "He knows that no one's ever thought of him as a good cop, that he's been the butt of everyone's jokes his whole life. He wanted to prove everyone wrong. So he took the animals and assigned himself the case to finally get some credibility in this town. He even took a cat from Pritchett, since he was trying to make the case seem more important by making it bigger, and he thought that might cast some of the suspicion off himself. He cooked meat for the animals, since he didn't want to arouse suspicion at the pet food store. One thing, though, and I believe him on this—he swears he never took your cat."

Callowe and Alby came out a few minutes later. Alby was clearly crushed. His face was tear-stained and his chest heaved up and down. I actually felt sorry for him, though I wanted our cat back.

"You're positive he doesn't have Zayde?" I asked Gus.

"I'm sure. Now why don't you two take Yoda and Fonzie back to their owners," Gus said. "Callowe and I will return the other one to Pritchett." He walked across the lawn with Fluffy under his arm, toward Callowe's police car.

We drove to Mackenzie's house to drop off Yoda first—I was glad to return Yoda to her, though I didn't know what to say about the whole Colin thing. I guessed I had to figure out some way to make peace with her. It wasn't her fault that I was so slow to figure out what I felt about Colin, that I had lost my chance.

I held Yoda on my lap in the car. Fonzie sat in the back, barking out the window and occasionally chewing the edge of the seat.

As we pulled up the long driveway to Mackenzie's farm-house, my mouth opened. I couldn't believe what I saw.

"Is that Colin's minivan in the driveway?" Sam asked.

My voice crackled, "It is." I held Yoda tightly. She dug her claws into my jeans. Colin and Mackenzie were to-gether. At ten o'clock at night. I felt queasy, a thousand times worse than I had after the night of Long Island Iced Teas.

We knocked on Mackenzie's door. She opened it, and beamed. "Yoda!" She cuddled her cat in her arms, and hugged and kissed her, and spun around.

Colin appeared behind her. "Hey," he said.

"Hey," I said coldly. I tried to catch Mackenzie's eye— I hoped maybe she would tell me what was going on with them so at least it could be out in the open, but she didn't notice I was staring at her. She was too busy nuz-zling Yoda.

Sam explained what Alby had done, but Fonzie was still in the car, barking like mad. "We better get going— we've got to get him back to Troy," Sam said. "Before he eats through our entire backseat."

"Thanks so much, you guys," Mackenzie said, still fo-cused on Yoda. Colin scratched Yoda's head. Seeing Colin and Mackenzie next to each other, I felt so awful I couldn't even think. I didn't say anything.

"See you tomorrow," Colin said to me.

I shrugged and turned away, and Sam and I returned to our car.

"Is something wrong? Why are you so quiet?" Sam asked.

"It's nothing," I said. I didn't want to get into it now. "We just need to hurry and return Fonzie."

Troy wasn't home when we dropped Fonzie off, but his mom answered the door and Fonzie happily bounded inside and jumped on the couch.

"Thank you, girls," Troy's mom said. Her red hair was in curlers, and she wore a yellow bathrobe. "Troy will be so happy his amigo is back. Oh, Fonzie sweetie. Yes, Fonzarelli." Fonzie licked her all over, and she smiled. "Fonzie's home. Everything's all right again."

I wished I could've said the same thing. Just when we thought our country-music-song-worthy miseries couldn't get any worse, they had. Sam was exhausted when we got home and went right to sleep, but I lay in bed staring up at the ceiling. I didn't even want to write in my journal, since Colin had given it to me. Writing in it would just make me think about him, and make me feel even more depressed. Maybe we should just leave town. Maybe it would be easier for us to start over again.

Fourteen

I spent the next day in bed. Mackenzie and Colin had both left several phone messages, but I told Sam to just tell them that I was sick. The idea of Thanksgiving and the Turkeyluck on Thursday made me feel even worse. Thanksgiving, the holiday that's supposed to be filled with loved ones and family. My whole body felt heavy, thinking about it. I thought of the huge turkeys my dad used to roast, and the turkey à la king we'd hated. Now I wanted some like crazy. I sank more deeply under the covers.

"You're not really sick, are you?" Sam asked me Wednesday morning.

"Sick in the head," I mumbled from beneath the quilt.

"What's going on?" she asked me.

I poked my head out. "Maybe we should just pack up and move to Fiji. We can't stay here anymore."

"Are you thinking about Josh and Leo and Hertznick?"

I nodded, even though I'd meant that I had to get away from Colin and my best friend being in love. I still hadn't told Sam anything about it; discussing it out loud would just make me feel even more terrible. Hertznick's visit to Leo and Josh was a whole other set of woes.

"I've been thinking about what Difriggio said—that we should get closer to Leo and Josh—and, well, I just talked to Josh this morning. He and Leo are coming over in two hours."

I sat up. "What?"

"They're leaving today for Josh's parents' house in Chicago for Thanksgiving. I invited them to stop by on the way. I thought we should talk."

"Why? Are we going to tell them the truth?"

"I don't think we should state it that plainly. I just think it's a good idea to smooth things over. To let them know we trust them . . . or at least are going to try to trust them." She gazed at me. "So we can stay in Venice, then. No Fiji. At least not for a little while. Are you going to get out of bed now?"

My stomach warmed at the thought of seeing Leo and Josh again. I was pretty certain they'd be on our side—and if they were, then at least I had them, even if I didn't have Colin and Mackenzie anymore. "Okay," I said. "I'm getting up."

Two hours later, Leo and Josh sat on our sofa, drinking tea and eating cookies. I couldn't eat anything, I was so nervous about discussing the Hertznick episode and our real identities out in the open.

Sam told them about our trip to Vegas, and they laughed at the description of Schmelvis. I kept waiting for someone to mention the subject of Hertznick. Or maybe we'd just pretend forever that it hadn't happened, like the way Gus reacted after seeing Jack?

But finally, Leo put his teacup down and said, "I know

Josh told you about the private detective asking me if I knew anything about the Shattenberg sisters. During that conversation, I told Hertznick I knew nothing. But later, I had second thoughts and called Hertznick back."

My lungs tightened and the room swam.

"Hertznick said to call him if I heard anything from or about the two runaway sisters," he continued. "I called and told him I had."

I was certain I was about to have a heart attack. Sam shouldn't have invited them here. This was obviously a colossal mistake. She gripped the edges of the armchair so tightly, her knuckles turned white.

"I told him that another relative of mine in California received a call from the sisters, asking for help. The relative called me to ask if I knew who these sisters were, and I remembered Hertznick, so I thought I should pass on the update. I told him my relative said they were headed for South America."

My mouth dropped open. Leo *lied* for us? This whole time, Leo never acknowledged the obvious fact in the air—that Sam and I were the Shattenberg sisters. But he finished his story calmly, matter-of-factly.

"I simply thought you might find this interesting, since you're in the business of finding missing people."

Josh smiled. I didn't know what to say. Sam and I both sat there, completely stunned.

"We need to get going," Leo said, patting the pockets of his pants as he stood up. "I hope you both know that if you ever need me, or are ever in trouble, you can turn to me for help. Anytime, for any reason."

"Same with me," Josh said.

"Thanks—it's good to know that," Sam said quietly, a smile spreading across her face.

"Well, happy Thanksgiving," Josh said.

"Happy Thanksgiving." I hugged Leo, and then Josh. Sam hugged them, too, and then Josh kissed her, his lips lingering on her cheek, an inch from her mouth. Leo raised his eyebrows and I grinned. We looked away, trying to give them a little privacy.

Later that afternoon, we had another visitor. It was Mackenzie.

"Why haven't you been returning my calls?" she asked me. "What's wrong? Are you feeling any better?"

"Yeah, I'm feeling better today," I said. The thought of her and Colin together still bugged me, but I was relieved to have cleared the air with Josh and Leo.

She followed me up to my room and we sat on my bed. I didn't know how to ask her about Colin being at her house late on Monday night without sounding like a crazy jealous person. I mean, if things with her and Colin worked out, then I would have to accept it.

"Colin's worried about you, too," she said.

I shrugged coolly.

"Why are you so mad at him?" she asked.

"I'm not mad. I'm happy that you guys are together." I forced a smile.

Mackenzie looked at me as if I'd just declared I was a space alien. "What are you talking about?"

"The other night, at the video store and at your house, late . . ."

"Oh please. Do you know why he came over?"

I braced myself. I didn't want to hear the details of their romantic evening.

"He came over to talk about you. He wanted advice on what to do about *you*." She started to laugh. "I can't believe you thought he was interested in me."

I blinked at her. "What?"

"Colin's just a friend. Kinda like a brother-type friend, although nicer than my brother of course."

"But you said he'd make someone a great boy-friend . . ."

"Someone. Not *me*." She shook her head. "Where do you get these ideas?" She saw how relieved I was, and a smile crept over her face.

"He likes me, then? For real? I mean . . . like-like?"

She nodded. "Like-like. Now what are you going to do?"

Thanksgiving morning, Sam drove me to Kroger's before it closed to buy flour, sugar, oil, eggs, and yeast. Then I brought the ingredients over to Colin's shop. I knocked on the door.

"Sophie?" he asked. "What are you doing here?"

"You said you needed help making bread. I'm sure you don't want anyone to break another tooth on it, like Henry did last year."

I brought the shopping bag in and we went upstairs to his kitchen. It was pristinely clean since he barely ever used it; Colin lived off pizza and macaroni and cheese.

We set out the ingredients, proofed the yeast, and

measured out the flour, just as I used to do with my mom. I showed him how to knead it, and then we set it in a bowl on top of the refrigerator to rise.

"What kind of bread is this?" he asked.

"Brioche," I said. "We're going to shape it into rolls." I thought if I made it in a traditional braid or round loaf, it would be too obvious that it was challah. As the bread rose, we returned to the comfortable couches in his shop, which he'd closed for the holiday. The Boggle set sat on a shelf. A thin layer of dust had grown on top of it.

"Did Mackenzie tell you I talked to her about . . . stuff?"

"Um . . . I . . ." I wasn't sure what to say.

"I should never have bugged either of you guys with all that—it was just stupid. I think we should just go back to the way things were before," he said. "That's what I've been thinking. I should never have tried to change things in the first place. I don't know. I mean—I think we should go back to the way things were before." He finally stopped babbling and just nodded.

"Okay," I said, though something in me sank. The whole Mackenzie thing had made me realize that I did want something more. But I didn't want to push things either.

The bread doubled in bulk and then we punched it down again. We set it out for a second rising and played a round of Boggle. I don't know if he was distracted, or tired, or what, but I beat him by twenty-six points.

By four o'clock the Petal Diner was teeming with people and dishes of food. Wilda repeatedly checked on the two massive turkeys and put finishing touches on her pies. There were eight different pies laid out on the counter. "I've got peach rhubarb, peach strawberry, strawberry rhubarb, strawberry rose, blueberry, pumpkin, pecan, and a new recipe I just invented—frangipane and rose."

Henry, who worked in the cafeteria at Venice High, asked, "Franjy-who?"

"It's a mixture of almond paste, sugar, and lots of good things. You'll love it," Wilda said.

"What did you bring?" I asked Henry.

He pointed to a huge brown appliance imprinted with FAT-O-MATIC sitting on the counter. "I'm making hush puppies," he said. "It's an old family recipe."

Wilda looked worried. "Can't you just use my deep fryer?"

He shook his head. "No way. The Fat-O-Matic is the secret. You have to eat 'em while they're hot. Wilda won't let me plug it in yet."

More people arrived with their casserole dishes wrapped in foil. Wayne of the pet store had brought a Tofurkey. He'd also given Gerard Moncrief a ride over.

"Double double toil and trouble, fire burn and cauldron bubble, et cetera, what do we have here?" Moncrief asked, peeking into a deep pot.

"Chicken soup," Wilda said. She surveyed all the food coming in. Fern brought Sea Foam Jell-O Salad, which was a neon blue. Gus brought a Cheddar cheeseball coated in walnuts. He'd put on his plaid suit for the occasion. He was looking much better than he had in weeks as he handed the cheeseball to Wilda. Did this mean Jack was coming? Jack hadn't written back to me since the last e-mail, but maybe he'd written to Gus.

"You look good," I told him. "Is . . . um?"

"Yes?" Gus asked.

"Um . . . nothing." I didn't want to bring up a sore subject in case Gus hadn't heard from him.

"What's happening with Alby?" Sam asked Gus and Wilda, changing the subject.

Wilda sighed. "We've talked about pressing charges—Fern wanted to, but Mackenzie and Fred just felt sorry for Alby, and frankly I do, too. Troy wanted to press charges at first, but then he realized that might not be so smart considering he's been in trouble with Alby and Callowe before for underage drinking. Vera Castleberry over in Pritchett also forgave him. Everyone knows Alby's a misguided fellow. He's apologized to everyone and swears he'll never do anything like this again. He's also agreed to do community service at Ergaster's animal shelter."

"Only in Venice does the town let a cop who's committed a crime completely off the hook," Gus said.

"That's what makes Venice so special," Wilda said. "And anyway, it's Thanksgiving." She turned toward the doorway, and grinned at what she saw.

It was Jack. He looked stunningly handsome in a perfectly fitted Italian suit, the antithesis of what Gus was wearing.

Gus breathed in deeply and smoothed his plaid

jacket. Jack was swarmed by Wilda, Wayne, and Moncrief. Wilda hugged and kissed him and started offering him appetizers, and Wayne gave him a massive hug. Moncrief shouted, "Crikey, you've turned into a dapper gent!"

Jack looked around the crowd, saw us standing next to his dad, and made his way over. He and Gus shook hands.

"Thanks for your e-mail," he said to Gus.

"Thanks for yours," Gus told him.

"You e-mailed Gus—?" I asked hesitantly.

"I decided I'd just say hello. That was it, really. But then he wrote me back," Jack said.

"I apologized for how I acted in Vegas," Gus said. He and Gus stared at each other for a long minute. "Glad you could come," Gus said, and patted him once on the back.

"I didn't want to miss another Turkeyluck." He eyed Gus's plaid suit. "You look nice," he said, attempting to sound truthful.

I tried to stifle a smile.

"You don't like this? Women used to love this suit," Gus said.

"In nineteen seventy-five," I said.

Jack and Sam laughed. "Should we grab seats?" Gus asked.

The three of them sat down, but I wanted to go find Colin. "I'll join you in a minute," I said. "Maybe you should keep an eye on them," I whispered to my sister. "They might need a buffer."

She nodded. "Good idea."

Colin was rearranging our "brioche" rolls on the table—they looked beautiful, golden and glistening. Henry announced, "It's time to fry my puppies." He set the Fat-O-Matic on the counter and plugged it in.

"That fryer really looks kinda old." Wilda bit her lip. "Can't you just use mine?"

"No," Henry said. "The Fat-O-Matic is the best in the—"

He paused midsentence, because everything went dark.

Murmurs of "What—? What happened?" rose from the crowd.

"It's okay!" Wilda yelled. "Everyone remain calm! It's probably just a short circuit—I've got some flashlights and candles somewhere!"

She jostled around and finally found a flashlight that worked. "Everyone remain calm!" she shouted again, but her own voice sounded panicky. She said that the diner shared a circuit breaker with the hardware store next door, and asked if anyone would volunteer to go down to the basement, where it was located. Colin's voice rose beside me. "I'll do it."

"I'll help you," I told him.

Wilda handed us the flashlight, and we bumped through the kitchen and to the basement door, carefully navigating our way down the long, dark staircase. Colin held my elbow. "Careful," he said. I slowly went down each dark step.

We wandered through the basement. It was dark and

cavernous, filled with cobwebs and dust. Colin flashed the light around. The corridors looked like they went on and on. "Tunnels connect the basements of all the stores on Main Street," he said. "They were built over a hundred years ago. The same family used to own all of them."

We walked along the basement's wall, keeping close to each other. I tripped over something, and he grabbed my hand. After I steadied myself, he kept holding my hand in his. A chill traveled through me and settled on my skin.

We kept wandering until we reached a passageway into another room. "I think this goes to the hardware store," he said. Then he stopped. "Did you hear that?"

"What?" I listened closely. It was a strange, scratching sound. Then it went away.

We walked down the passage and into the next basement. Colin shone his light along the wall, looking for the circuit breaker.

Then I heard it again. It wasn't scratching. It was coughing. Colin shined his flashlight around the room until it shone on a pair of bright green eyes.

"Zayde!" I called out. She trotted toward me. She was much skinnier than she had been when I'd last seen her. She rubbed against my ankles and purred. I picked her up and hugged her to my chest. She was covered in dust and spiderwebs. "How did she get down here?"

"She must have gotten in through an opening on the street," Colin said. "Maybe a loose vent or manhole or something." He scratched her behind the ears, and she purred even louder.

Colin pointed his light at a panel of circuit breakers. "Here it is." He fiddled with them for a few minutes, and after he flicked several switches, a distant cheer rose from upstairs.

"I think that did it," he said, and laughed.

We started walking back toward the staircase leading to the Petal. Colin picked up my hand again as we walked, holding it gently, gingerly lacing his fingers through mine. His hand was soft and warm. My heart pounded. A strange tickle rose in my belly. We walked toward the stairs. A stripe of yellow light glowed below the doorframe at the top.

Colin paused at the base of the staircase and switched off his flashlight. He turned to face me in the darkness. Without saying a word, he gathered me toward him, Zayde sandwiched between us, and his lips melted into mine.

"I'm staying," I whispered in a haze.

"What?"

"I mean—" I didn't have to explain or say anything else, because he gathered me into another kiss.

Acknowledgments

I'm grateful to Jackie Rabb for patiently reading endless drafts and answering my ridiculous questions. A special thank you to Ben Schrank for publishing my first story ever, and to Sara Shandler, a dream editor, for her constant enthusiasm and good cheer. And thank you to Marshall Reid, for everything.

Don't miss the other books in this exciting series!

Missing Persons book one: The Rose Queen

Missing Persons book two: The Chocolate Lover

WANTED

...for a special television appearance!

NAME: Sophie Shattenberg

AGE: 15

DETAILS: Wanted to appear in a special episode of *Griffin on the Go!*

Sam and Sophie have built new lives for themselves in Venice, Indiana, and things seem to be going smoothly. That is, until Sophie slips up and gives Wilda—the owner of their favorite hangout, the Petal Diner—her mother's matzo ball soup recipe. Before she knows it, Wilda has put her own midwestern touches on the recipe, entered it into a cooking contest, and won first prize!

Wilda will have the chance to appear on her favorite show—*Griffin on the Go!*—and she wants Sophie to be on the show with her. Sophie knows she can't risk having her face broadcast on television, but when Wilda and the show's host disappear, she finds that she has bigger things to worry about....

Read M. E. Rabb's next Missing Persons novel:

The Unsuspecting Gourmet

Coming soon!